Dear America

When Christmas Comes Again

The World War I Diary of Simone Spencer

BY BETH SEIDEL LEVINE

Scholastic Inc.   New York

New York City
1917

April 6, 1917

Dear Diary,

There. I've always wanted to write that. I wonder how it is that in all these years, with all these thoughts and so many daydreams, I've never put pen to paper. Well, now I must. We are at war. This, on Good Friday, no less!

Practically the whole world has been at war for years and now our own President Wilson has brought America into the fight. We've joined the Allied forces against the Kaiser in Germany on this day. I suppose it all sounds very exciting in some ways.

It's funny. A moment ago, I didn't know what I should do with my life once high school was finished. I've been feeling so very useless. Now in some strange way, I feel like perhaps being at war will change that. Perhaps I will find myself somewhere in it.

April 9

In just one weekend, it seems the whole world has changed. Everywhere there is talk of the war and what it means. Already, there is a call for volunteers of all kinds.

Here at our house, though, things are quite the same. Yesterday was Easter Sunday, so my brother, William, came for supper with Caroline. She is his wife and although she is rather pesky in her society ways, I do believe she means well. It is strange to me that Will chose someone like her. I suppose we are society, too. I mean, by our name, Spencer, we are. But, Maman would not have us presume to act it.

She is French, my Maman. And she is beautiful and fine. She married Father because he bought every last croissant in her mother's bakeshop when he was on holiday in Paris one summer. She always tells us the story on their anniversary.

Father starts first. He's the romantic. Funny, isn't it? That he, the American after all, is the one with his eyes filled with moonlit love, and that she, the lovely French girl, barely moons at all? I think it's perfectly wonderful actually. Maman always says things work out better when they go the opposite way of what is expected.

So the story goes this way. Having gotten lost in Paris, Father walked into the pâtisserie (I try to use French on occasion to please Maman) owned by Maman's family to ask for directions. According to Father, he stopped the moment he walked through the door, realizing that he might already love the *very* beautiful, *very* much immersed in a book, Maman.

She, on the other hand, looked up from her book when the bells at the top of the door jingled, only to find a very English-looking American boy nervously searching for some French to impress her. Although many English-looking American boys commonly appeared when those bells at the top of the door jingled, he was the first such boy she found herself smiling at. In spite of herself.

But it was when he told her he would buy every last croissant in the shop that she knew she would always smile for him.

In telling the story, neither Father nor Maman ever continues beyond that point. They never tell the part about the disgrace Father's parents suffered when their terribly eligible son chose to marry an ordinary (to them only, I assure you), French girl instead of one of the many well-bred, well-moneyed, young women that would have secured their place in the high society of New York City. And they don't tell the part about Maman returning with Father at the end of that summer after a very private wedding (Father and Maman only), which left my dear Grandparents no choice but to announce the news properly and put on their happiest faces to all. But never to Maman.

And so, we live somewhat differently from the others. Oh, we attend many of the parties, give dinners from time to time, and chat merrily with the ladies at Maman's hat shop. But we rarely take them seriously, and we never drink tea. Maman thinks tea has no soul and that café au lait is heaven on earth.

We were all rather surprised, then, when Will announced his intention to marry Caroline Lawson — society girl extraordinaire! But we have found that underneath all those fashionable clothes and upper-class airs is a girl who loves Will very much. So we love her, too.

April 15

What a glorious day! Have I mentioned Frances? I call her Francie and she is my best friend in the world. There is nothing we like better than to spend an entire day roaming around our own New York City. We try to walk as much as we can but Father still insists that Max follow us around in the car just in case. Our most favorite thing of all is to go to Central Park. Today, Sally (she's our cook, whom I adore) packed us a basket full of treats, so we had a picnic in a rowboat on the pond. We just sat there lounging and admiring the scene. There were so many fine-looking women (and men, too!).

Oh, and the hats, I just love hats. They say that you are practically undressed if you step outside without one. And that's just fine with me. Maman has her very own hat shop, simply called Brigitte (her own name), where she designs the hats for all the ladies in town. She became a chapelier because she simply would not sit around all day with nothing to do.

Francie and I stopped in at the shop after the park and tried on each and every hat in the place. I particularly like the ones that have come out recently with one single feather sticking straight up from the front. How outrageous! In the end, we were glad that Max was nearby so we could collapse into the backseat and watch the city go by through the window on our way home.

I know that people live all over this country. I know

that there are beautiful farmlands in the middle of the country, majestic mountains in the West. And I know that people spend their days walking down Main Street in small towns all over the map. I know that there are other big cities, with a bustle all their own, to be sure. I know all of this, but I simply cannot imagine it. I cannot imagine a world outside of this one, a city better-lived in, than my own.

Well, perhaps Paris.

April 17

Not too much to write about really, but I am trying desperately to be disciplined about keeping a diary. I thought I would sit in the lovely writing chair Father gave me for my seventeenth birthday. (My birthday falls on the first day of every new year. A fresh start all around — what luck!) Father knows how much I love reading and so he presumed I would love writing just as much. I hadn't thought of it myself. Truth be told, I'd much rather someone else do the writing for me.

However, I've started to try to think up some stories to write and I'll say only this for it: There is something awfully appealing about deciding the way things go. Yes, there is something nice indeed about making sure that everything goes as you'd want it to. For now, I'll write down events as they happen for real and save the story writing for when things don't go my way!

So, instead of sitting in that lovely writing chair, I sit on my sofa near the fireplace, which makes my room my very favorite place. My second favorite place is the kitchen because that is where the women cook up delicious dinners and extravagant plans. Sally always has the most marvelous plans of them all. With her, Francie, Maman, and I are not society girls at all. With her, we plot to steal away on one of the giant ships that sits on the waterfront waiting for cargo. We think it a waste for those ships to sail without people aboard to enjoy the sea air and look forward to far-off destinations. So we plan to wait until dark and then sneak off, out into the streets where we run in our nightclothes and boots — skipping and dancing. And while all the neighbors sleep in their stodgy beds, dreaming of luxurious cruise ships, Sally, Francie, Maman, and I stow away in the underbelly of a ship bound for the islands . . . where adventures await!

I love the kitchen. And I love my spot in it — right in

the corner of the counter where I hoist myself up and let my feet dangle while we tell stories and sample Sally's treats.

But in my room, I am happiest. It is the perfect size. Big enough to let my mind wander around a bit, small enough to keep me from losing track of it.

April 20

Francie's mother, Mrs. Walker, isn't like mine at all. I imagine that is why Francie spends so much time with us, and heaven knows I couldn't be more pleased about that. Francie should really be an actress. She has fiery red hair and a personality to match! She is everything I am not. For one, she is as funny as can be. This drives her mother mad since Francie's particular kind of funny — silly funny, side-splitting funny — isn't becoming of a lady in search of a proper husband. Francie agrees (with a wink). I think she's quite clever being so silly — now she won't have to be the wife of a proper husband. Maybe she won't have to be a wife at all.

Boys in uniform already populate the streets, and I wish there were no war.

May 2

I don't have very much to write these days. School is finishing up and I am feeling terribly bored. I plan to look into volunteering (doing what, I don't know) the moment school ends.

For now, I sit here trying to think up a story to write. Each time I begin, I crumple that paper up and toss it in the trash bin. Perhaps I do this to feel more like a writer. Isn't that what they always do? Write something and promptly toss it in the trash?

May 7

I have been wanting school to be finished for such a long time and now that we are in the last month of it, I am anxious about what will lie ahead. I don't know why I have found school to be so uninteresting. Arithmetic I could certainly do without, and Latin, well that's another story. My parents thought that surely I would excel in it since I have grown up speaking French. But I have not done well at all! It is much too serious a subject for my taste. I do like to read, though. And I love to learn. I simply have trouble sitting still for it.

Until this year, I never gave a thought to what would come next. There was always something set up for me. Now, my life stretches out in front of me and I long for a sign to come crashing down from the heavens. Otherwise, I think I shall hole up in my room for the rest of my life, just like depressed old Emily Dickinson. They say she was at one time an energetic soul, but that once she had finished school, she took to her house. Some say she had to remove herself from life in order to write so intimately about it.

An odd analysis, I think. I sit down to write the stories of my life and I think myself terribly presumptuous. Don't you have to have lived some stories of your own before you can write them down?

May 12

Francie talks incessantly of the Women's Suffrage Movement. She thinks we ought to be able to vote. She's always felt like that, since we were very little girls. She was always wandering into adult conversations as if she were meant to be there with them, as if she were not a ten-year-old girl with ribbons in her hair, as if she should be in the thick of it with them, smoking on a pipe, lamenting the state of city politics.

She has very little restraint and even less tact. I wish I could be more like that. I wish I could say just what I feel at the very moment I feel it. Instead, I am a bit quiet, a bit reluctant to break the rules. We make a nice pair that way. Sometimes, I think that if I were not around for Francie, she would find herself sitting in the city jail for sneaking into the movies without paying. And if I had no Francie, I would find myself sitting calmly in my seat at the theater with a fully paid ticket instead of with the fast heartbeat that comes from evading the ushers! Life would be dull without Francie.

May 18

This is the latest on the war front. All males between the ages of twenty-one and thirty are required to register for military service. That includes Will.

Father tries very hard to keep the world nice and safe for me, so I didn't know too much about why we went to war or what it meant. I knew what I had read in the paper and what I overheard while lurking outside Father's study when his friends were over, but until the President actually declared war, the war in Europe might as well have not been going on at all for me. That's the problem around here. We all go about our business in a bit of a daze. Francie is right. If women were expected to vote, maybe we would pay closer attention to what is going on in the world and less attention to what so and so wore to last week's main event.

So I took Francie up on her challenge and did some research. Well, not research really. All I did was ask Father to explain to me how it is that we've gotten into a war with Germany when I don't notice Germany doing anything to harm us here in America. Of course, for Maman alone, I'm glad we've gotten into it with them, since they've advanced on her beloved Paris. I hope we protect that city. I haven't been there yet.

Father explained that although we haven't been attacked directly, the Germans have threatened us by breaking their pledge to limit submarine warfare. (This sounds very serious to me.) When they did that, President Wilson refused to have diplomatic relations with Germany any longer. And then there was the Zimmerman telegram. It was published in the papers in March, and for weeks this was all anyone could talk about, but I didn't realize what it really meant. Father told me that that telegram was intercepted by the British on its way from Germany to Mexico. When the British decoded it, they discovered that Germany had intended to entice Mexico to join in the fight in exchange for Germany's help in getting Mexico some United States territory! Well, I guess that awoke us.

Father and I had a good chat about the whole thing and I feel better informed now. Francie's right. Suddenly, I wish I had some more control.

May 25

My dear brother, William, volunteered for the army this day. He will not wait to be called by draft. He thinks that's not the patriotic thing to do. Perhaps not, but I'd prefer it anyway.

Early this afternoon, he asked me to go for an ice cream, and when I told him that I had planned to go over to the YMCA to volunteer, he suggested that it was more important that I spend the afternoon with him. I suspected his news and thought for a moment about ignoring his wishes just to put off hearing it for a bit longer, but I thought I'd better take the time with him while I could.

Also, the winter has finally thawed and the air has that smell that always makes me wish I could suck as much of it into my lungs as possible and store it there for when it gets stale again. Then, on a bitter cold afternoon in dreary February, I would blow it all out and fill my room with Spring instead.

So I went with him.

And now as the spring air blows through my window, I can hardly suck in even a breath of it.

This Great War isn't great at all, is it?

May 26

Caroline is all but a wreck. I suspect Maman is, too, but when Will told her, she just put on her smile and made him give her an extra long hug. Maman is a fascinating woman, you know. She does not get hysterical like so many other mothers I know (Mrs. Walker for one). She does not put up fights over little things like what is proper and what is not.

And today I realized something about her, which I think I admire most in her. She trusts us. Of course she doesn't want Will to go to war, but she knows her son — knows that once Will has made up his mind, that is the end of the discussion. And he wants to go, so why waste the time arguing?

Don't think she isn't full of emotion, though. It just comes out in other ways. Like when her temper gets hot if Father even smiles kindly at another woman at a party. Or when she blushes when he brings her a bucket filled with fresh-cut lilies of the valley the next day. And then when her eyes fill up when we're all sitting around the dining room table together chatting and laughing. She's filled with all the right emotions, my Maman.

May 27

We've just come from dinner at the Grandparents and I am exhausted. I always am after a night with Grandmother — I do believe most people are. And what I have never understood is why she insists on being so very tiring. It seems so contrary to what she otherwise is, for she is such a fine woman. So lovely in appearance, with the very best wardrobe in town and the very best manners. Very old-time fashionable. She seems so wise, but is so terribly stuck in her old-time ways.

I imagine she likes to pretend that the borders of Gramercy Park are the borders of the world, and that nothing ever changes. Father says she prefers to live in a world where all the last names are either Dutch or English, where money matters are left to the men (who have inherited large sums, not really *earned* it), and where girls do not want (and certainly do not need) an education in anything other than the fine art of manners. This matter is where she and I have our particular tensions.

"Honestly, Simone," she said the moment I walked through the door, "wherever did you find that dress? A young girl like yourself ought to be wearing something that *attracts* young men. Perhaps if you'd spend more time with your head in the hands of my hair dresser and less time with it stuck in a book, you'd be engaged by now." Then she shot a false smile at Maman and said, "Well, what could I expect really?" Grandmother blames Maman for practically every matter that irks her so — the fact that Father became a physician instead of taking over his father's real estate investment businesses; the fact that I do not come by social grace naturally (I've never understood this one, since Maman is far more gracious than I could ever be); and now the fact that Maman would not let the Grandparents find a way for Will to avoid his service in the war. Father wouldn't let them either, but to them it's Maman's fault. Naturally.

Next Grandmother turned her attention to Will and Caroline. "Ah, there they are, the future of the family, indeed!" She took Caroline's hands and looked her up and down with approval. "Simone, won't you take a lesson from Caroline, darling? Don't you want to find yourself on the arm of a young man just like William?" She didn't wait for any kind of answer, of course. She never does. We simply followed her like soldiers to the dining room where I had to endure more of the usual comments about my appearance, about the fact that I read too much, about my wanting to be useful in life. "But, Simone dear, you'll be plenty useful to your husband in managing his home, planning his parties, and giving him children who will continue his name." By that point in the meal, I had lost my will to fight her, so I smiled and told her I'd be sure to give it some thought.

Grandfather is another matter. The same way Grandmother spends the evening picking on me, he spends his time picking on Father. Although lately, he seems to have given up on Father altogether and has turned his attention to Will, whom he hopes will help revive the family's real estate business. Somehow Will endures him — has been enduring him for a few years now, as Will has agreed to learn the business and give it a try. I wonder why their life appeals to him so much more than it does me. I do think Father is relieved that Will's interest has taken the pressure off of him. I also think he's pleased that Will is to Grandfather what he never wanted to be — an heir.

We all breathed a sigh of relief the moment we stepped outside. Caroline even gave me a smile and then she did the funniest thing. In this exaggerated way, she said, "Really Simone, we must get you some decent dresses, daaahling!" I let out such a laugh. I didn't know Caroline could be so incorrigible! Then with a wink she said good-bye and left for home with my brother. I supposed Grandmother's compliments embarrass her the same way the insults embarrass me.

I am so bothered by the Grandparents because I just don't see things their way. And I'm not sure why their views are so limited. You see, I dress rather well, I think. With Maman's fabulous taste, why wouldn't I? But Grandmother just refuses to believe that I could embrace some of the things from her world, and at the same time dismiss others that don't suit me. Perhaps she wishes she would have dismissed some of them herself.

May 28

Will is off to basic training! I suppose I hadn't considered that he would have to train first before going off to war. I know I should be sad to see him go, but I am laughing at the idea of him running all around to get fit, lining up, and answering to a superior officer shouting his name at the crack of dawn! He was angry with me for pointing this out to everyone this morning. He was even angrier when the whole lot of us started laughing at the idea. Even Caroline!

Will thinks that because he is a good athlete (and he is) he will make a good soldier. Say what you will about society folk. One thing I know with certainty is that they couldn't possibly make good soldiers.

I apologized to Will for making fun. I told him we had to laugh hard now, because we will be crying even harder when he leaves for Europe. He relaxed then and we set about getting him some stationery to write home with.

Later

I have two examinations next week and I haven't begun to study. It will be a late night . . .

June 3

A letter from Will already. He says he's having a good old time. I suspect he's making himself look good so we are not proven correct! His only complaint was that they have him taking French lessons of all things. And from an American. Maman was not impressed. He says he's hoping to get out of it.

One more exam to go and then I graduate. To what?

June 8

I did miserably on my Latin exam, but I hardly care. I did so well all year long (in all my *other* subjects) I don't think it matters. Besides, what good could Latin do in the world anyway? I have plenty of other skills that will help me along. I just have to figure out what they are.

June 19

Will is home, but only for a week! He just missed my graduation. I should have written about it that day, but some days I'm so lazy I have a staring contest with my diary instead of writing in it. On those days, I convince myself that I'll remember everything the next time I write. Only, when I pick it up again, I have forgotten most every detail.

Like now, all I can remember is that I graduated, we came back to the house for lunch, and I opened gifts. Maman had given me a hat early that morning that was absolutely divine. It was made of tightly woven brown straw with a wide brim, laced with a fat dark chocolate ribbon. It was perfect with my brand new chocolate linen dress. Grandmother gave me a subscription to *The Ladies' Home Journal*. She's tried this tactic over and over with Maman. She'll never give up.

Father gave me a sterling silver writing pen with a note that said *Whatever lies ahead, keep a record of it.* I suppose I'm an even worse person for not writing that very night since I had such a lovely new instrument to write with!

June 24

Will's leaving. He ships out the day after tomorrow and I'm afraid I'm not handling the news very well. The papers show horrible pictures of the war, and I just hope Will understands what he's doing. I know I made jokes about it, but, really, he will have to be a soldier over there in the trenches. He'll have to be a different person entirely.

June 26

Today was quite something. It's taken me until now (must be near midnight) to collect myself enough to write legibly. Even still, I hiccup with residual sadness when I think of Will waving good-bye so cheerfully, so optimistically. "The war will be over by Christmas," he promised.

We took him to the seaport where there were absolutely throngs of people crowded around. Oh, to see all those good-byes! It was so sad. I will say, though, that something about it was comforting as well. All those boys in uniform, bravely boarding that big ship for Europe. They are off to fight and do you know that not one of them looked frightened? Inspiring, I tell you.

So, I was standing holding Caroline's hand with my right one and Maman's hand with my left as Will walked up the plank. Father had his arm around Maman on the other side. It was very serene. Maman was holding back tears with her smile and Caroline was, too, although I did feel her body shaking a bit. Then, suddenly, she broke free of our little chain and ran right up to the side of the plank shouting Will's name. I couldn't believe the drama! Well, Will played right along. He ran directly over to her and, bending down over the railing, pulled her up to him and gave her a kiss. They looked at each other for a long moment and then they let go.

We watched as the ship pulled away, all of us shouting and cheering. Caroline stood all by herself right by the water's edge for a long while, until Maman finally went to her and brought her back to us. Then Father took us all for a grand lunch, where we pretended that nothing was different. Nothing at all.

June 27

Today Francie came over to hold my head while I cried some more and we ended up laughing! Sally must have let her in because there I was sobbing like a mad woman into my pillow, wallowing in my own dreariness, when I heard stomping steps coming down the hallway — marching steps, actually. Then I heard singing, "Over there, Over there . . ." Francie had dressed up in one of my father's suits and a driving cap, making herself into a soldier — she had even drawn a mustache!

"The Yanks are coming, the Yanks are coming!" she continued. I sat up and stared at her, partly hoping she would quiet down and partly wishing she would never stop singing. Finally, I gave up all my crying for good and joined in. I even grabbed the hat from her head and hopped up on the bed, marching with all my heart. There we were singing and yelling at the top of our lungs when Sally came in to see what the commotion was. "Oh Sal," Francie begged her. "Come march with us, too." And she did! She got right up on that bed of mine and sang even louder until we all fell into a heap of hysterics.

Suddenly everything looks brighter. I wonder how it is for Will. How far across the ocean can he be in just two days?

Later

I must say this one thing. Though I am proud of my brave older brother, and worried for him, too, I realize that I am also rather envious of his lot as a man. I feel so strong, and yet I must be content to simply adhere to war rationing rules, volunteer locally, and go to Juliana Gardner's "Support Our Troops" party tomorrow evening. Girl's things, all of them. And it's not that I want to shoot off a gun or anything like that. It's simply this: When this is all over, when the Germans have pushed back and the boys come home, when the world gets back to normal, I'd like to have done more than forego meat on Wednesday nights.

Yet, here I sit. All the way across the grand Atlantic Ocean, all the way over here in good old New York City. And as much as they tell me that my efforts here on the home front matter, when I walk out my front door, I cannot escape the feeling that it doesn't feel like we're at war at all. But we are.

June 29

I went to Juliana's party. It was supposed to be a commencement party since we finally graduated this week. But Juliana doesn't think it makes much sense to celebrate while a war is going on, so she's turned it into a party for the troops. It was all too glamorous to be a war party no matter what she called it. After all, we had on our very best clothes and their home is simply beautiful.

The Gardners have the finest home any of us have seen. It is on "Millionaire's Row" on Fifth Avenue. And even though most of us have plenty of nice things and very fine homes, too, theirs is of a different class entirely. Maman even made me wear a corset! She never makes me wear one anymore — we've decided once and for all they are terrible. But, Mr. Gardner is rather important around this town and some people just have not changed with the changing times (that's what Father always says). So, I endured it. (Maman did not pull those strings very tight so it wasn't dreadful really — just silly.)

The house is, quite simply, enormous, with a *grand* reception hall and a *grand* staircase, down which Juliana herself glided, making her *grand* entrance once we'd all arrived. It was all just perfectly *grand*. Oh, please excuse my sarcasm, but I must say I find Juliana to be kind of a bore in all of her absolute *grandness*.

Anyway, the party itself was very nice, which made everything seem as usual. And, everyone wanted to know how Will was doing so that was very nice, too. Some of the boys from school have joined up, and they wanted to know what it was like. I have no details of course, but I admit the attention was appreciated! Mostly, Francie and I sat around gossiping about the others. Oh, we are terrible people. May God forgive us!

Off to sleep now.

July 1

I've decided to volunteer with the YMCA. I went today and found that there are all sorts of things to do. Even if I just collect donations and make gift packages for the soldiers, at least I'm doing *something*.

Most everyone is away for the summer but we prefer to stay in the city (oppressive as it can be). We do make some trips to visit friends out in the country, but Maman enjoys the "off season" right here, without the noise of all the parties and gossip. She always says summer gives us all a little extra freedom. Freedom from layers of clothing and strict schedules. That cold weather keeps us very tied up indeed!

July 4

We are in Newport visiting the Lawsons for the July Fourth holiday. We've been here since Saturday morning, lazing around on the lawn and making nice for tea each afternoon. Maman is so lovely to Mrs. Lawson, that I sometimes wish I could be more like her. I have trouble doing things I don't like to do. I wish we could be having café au lait on ice cubes instead of a "light, summer tea." Every once in a while, Maman shoots me a look — a funny face — that makes these idle afternoons more bearable. She is so very easygoing.

Caroline has been sweet to me, which is a treat. We've taken to acting more like sisters than sisters-in-law. I admit that it is nice to be here. I feel far away from the world out here and right now, that is just fine with me.

July 16

I think Maman wishes I would be a bit more social. She thinks I've gotten much too serious since the war has been on and that I ought to enjoy myself more. I know that the other girls my age are enjoying the summer on Long Island or in Newport, attending parties, meeting dashing young men. (I will admit only on these pages that perhaps that part appeals to me somewhat.) But really, how can they go on as if the world has not changed? I just can't join in the fun this summer. My time at the YMCA is the only time I feel useful, or at least a little less anxious.

Before this month, there were no women involved with the organization, but now service is open to women as well and YMCA offices are opening all over. One of the women there told me that within weeks of America's declaration of war, women living in France had already begun to operate Y canteens in Paris and Brest, France. They call them huts. Soldiers can go there to get basics like soap, toothbrushes, pencils, and things like that. They can also go to wet huts for some lemonade and cookies or a bowl of stew and maybe some hot chocolate when the weather turns cold. Here at the Y they feel that whatever they can do to make things easier on those boys, they happily will.

Later

I forgot to mention something that's been on my mind. At the commencement ceremony, Maddy Carlton came over to me and gave me a quick hug of congratulations. Do you know that she told me her older sister, Nancy, has joined the American Army as a nurse? I heard that nurses had gone over with the Red Cross. (I know a girl in the class ahead of mine whose sister was one of the first Americans to set foot in this war — before we actually entered the war, I mean.) But I certainly did not think that our own government would send girls to war. Maddy set me straight, indeed.

I wish I were a few years older so that I could be a nurse and go over to Europe right away. Now that I think of it, maybe that's not a bad idea at all. It would be a switch, to be sure. (At Father's suggestion, I have been giving some thought to attending college, but college just doesn't seem important enough right now.)

July 19

I've looked into nursing school and I believe it's just the thing for me. Maman agrees, although I believe she'd like me to put the notion off at least until the fall so that I might relax a while. I'm not sure it is in my nature to relax! I'm off to have a chat with Father about all this. (Crossing my fingers that he'll at least hear me out.) I do hope the fact that he is a physician will benefit me, for it is a compliment to him in a way.

Later

Father has agreed! Well, he's agreed to give it some thought anyway. I think he's finally gotten used to us not being like everyone else. I don't suppose he thought he'd have a daughter who was interested in living a life "of leisure." Not after marrying Maman. When I proposed that I register for nursing school, he seemed intrigued. I told him that I admired how he had dedicated his life to healing people and that I wished to do the same. He told me that he had hoped I would decide on college instead. (I did give serious thought to applying to one of the women's colleges in New England, but couldn't bear the thought of leaving New York City for school.) After a bit of pleading my case — well, a lot of pleading my case — he said that before I did anything terribly rash, I must start volunteering at the hospital where he works, instead of the YMCA. He said I wouldn't really know if nursing was for me until I had some "firsthand experience." I know nothing will make a difference in my decision, but I'll do it to humor him.

The name of the hospital where Father works is the Hospital for the Ruptured and Crippled. Isn't that awful?

July 20

Father did some thinking last night and decided that I should concentrate my volunteering efforts in a special ward the hospital has set up for soldiers who have (already) been wounded in the war. I'm thinking that's not a terrible idea. When Francie returns (have I mentioned she's been on holiday for two whole weeks?), I will ask her to go with me.

July 25

I've been sitting here with this book in my hand since I walked through my bedroom door. Yet it has taken me the better part of an hour to start writing today. I was fine all day until I closed the door behind me. Francie and I went to the hospital to volunteer, and it was all very good and interesting. We just helped out any way we could. Made bandage bundles, took inventory, things like that. Then one of the head nurses thought it might be a nice idea for us to visit with some of the recovering soldiers who had no family to visit them.

I couldn't imagine such a situation. Lying in a hospital after fighting a war and having no one come by to check on you. To make sure you made it out all right. How very sad. Well, we went into a room filled with injured dough-boys (that's what they're calling soldiers nowadays) and Francie went right to work. She introduced us to two young men lying side by side and said that we wanted to have a chat and get to know them a bit. One of them was very kind and cheerful and he and Francie got right to talking. It turned out that he *does* have a family — but they live in the South and couldn't come here right away.

But the other one, Thomas Stewart, he just lay there. His face was covered in dried-up scabs and his head was turned away from us. He had one leg up in traction. I tried several times to check in with him as Francie and the other boy (I regret that I cannot recall his name) chatted away. But Thomas just stared off into the air.

We left after about an hour and the head nurse asked us to come back any time. After I dropped Francie off, my mind started to wander. Will has all of us over here to worry about him every waking second. He has letters coming from home, a home that waits warmly here for him whenever he shall return. The thing is, that head nurse told us that Thomas has barely spoken a word since he arrived, and they have no next-of-kin information listed for him. She said he enlisted in the army even before the war began for us.

I came directly upstairs when I got home, and sobs came over me. Even now, the tears are wetting my cheeks. My eyes hurt and my heart hurts because any boy who goes over to that war and fights the good fight for this country ought to have better luck in his life than to come back terribly injured and find himself lying alone in a recovery ward.

And maybe I'm crying for Will, too. I'm not sure I've thought very much about the possibility of his being injured. Some of my sobbing must be that terrible reality coming over me from deep down in my belly. I think that's where I put my fear the night Will left.

Maybe nursing isn't for me after all.

July 28

A letter from Will at last!

He can't say much about where he is, but I must say

he sounds quite optimistic. He says Europe is divine and that I would like it very much (as if I didn't already know this)! He asked if I would get my hands on *The Sporting News* and send it over to him. Can you imagine? In the middle of a war he simply has to know how his sports teams are faring! I'll take it as good news.

July 31

I've been reading to try and pass the time while summer becomes hotter each day. Now more than ever, I feel like a waste of space. We haven't heard from Will again. I know he can't write every day, but still, I have nightmares about his condition. We keep hearing that this is a new kind of war. There is even chemical gas that destroys the lungs and a liquid called "mustard gas," which does damage to the skin and eyes as well as to the lungs. How strange to call it mustard gas — as if it might be a nice thing to put on your food!

I've been going to the hospital to help almost every day, but it doesn't seem enough. I am simply not meant to nurse people back to health. My plan has changed. I must find a way to go over there. To the war, I mean.

August 5

I sit with Thomas a little bit each day and he still says nothing to me — just stares off into the distance. But I stay with him because someone should, and because I don't know what else to do. I had a look at his chart this afternoon. Burned in an explosion in battle. Two broken legs.

What does he think about all day long?

August 19

A breakthrough! I've taken to bringing a book with me and reading aloud to Thomas in the afternoons. Well, I was nearly to the end of Dickens's *A Christmas Carol* (I thought it might do us a bit of good to be put in the mind of Christmas), and I had assumed all the while that he hadn't listened to a single word of it. But I was about to read the part where Scrooge has at last discovered the error of his ways, and has shown up at his nephew's house on Christmas Day, and has now endeavored to help Bob Cratchit by raising his salary and saving Tiny Tim. Yes, there I was about to read the very last line when Thomas turned his head to me and recited the whole of the line in unison with me. I looked at him but kept reading for fear that he would go back into his own world if I ever stopped reading. ". . . and it was always said of him, that he knew how to keep Christmas well, if any man alive possessed the knowledge. May that be truly said of us, and all of us! And so, as Tiny Tim observed, God Bless Us, Every One!" I tell you I never would have thought this Thomas was someone who would recite a novel from memory, but he did.

"Here I thought you weren't listening at all. I was beginning to think you a Scrooge, Thomas!" I said. "No," he said. "I was just waiting for the happy ending."

Well, with that, Thomas had opened the gates, let me tell you. He just started talking! He does have a family after all! The nurses were very excited to have some information at last. He ran away from home (right here in New York City) to join the army. He was a bit of a troublemaker and hated school so he had some problems with his parents. Since he was too young to join the army, he made up a name and age and said he had no family to speak of. Well, the nurses and I convinced him that we must telephone his parents at once. They must be sick with worry. He agreed.

I waited with Thomas until his parents arrived — the Brennans, not the Stewarts, since that was his invented name. The reunion was something else! Mrs. Brennan was absolutely shaking with relief and tears when she saw Thomas, and Mr. Brennan was consumed with the kind of tears men cry when they just can't hold it in any longer. After a few minutes, Mrs. Brennan turned to me and thanked me for staying with him, for helping him to come back to life, and for making him call them. She thanked *me*! I don't think I did anything at all. But my eyes welled up anyway. I slipped out of the room as the family reunion continued, leaving them to their moment.

August 28

I went to see Thomas today and he chastised me for leaving the other day. He said he was afraid he wouldn't see me again and he wanted to thank me, too. He was in such good spirits! And what a miraculous recovery he is suddenly making. He told me that he was feeling better and that soon enough his cast would be off and he would be off, too. He wouldn't say where he was going, though.

I am so glad I stayed with him. So glad I didn't run away.

September 7

I'm pleased that Thomas has finally come around, but I'm feeling a little lost again without the challenge of trying to break his silence. What shall I do now?

September 23

Thomas improves with every passing day. He no longer has scabs around his face and I can see now that he is quite handsome. There is a woman named Katherine who comes by to help him walk properly now that his leg is healed — she calls it "reconstruction." She was trained in England where this kind of therapy is much more common. Sometimes, I just sit and watch them go through the exercises because it is very satisfying to watch as she helps Thomas to independence. She must feel satisfied each and every day.

Thomas has finally revealed his mysterious plans. He intends to go all the way to Hollywood, California, in the hopes of one day becoming an actor in the movies!

I suppose I could see that. Yes, I would most certainly go to see a picture starring Thomas Stewart — I mean, Brennan.

October 8

Thomas has gone. When I got to the hospital today, Katherine told me that he was discharged and that he left in quite a hurry. No one knew where he had gone to, though. I believe I have an idea about that. But why wouldn't he at least say good-bye to me?

October 15

Will doesn't say much in his letters. He can't really say where he is, so he describes the countryside and some of his friends. It actually sounds like fun the way he writes. They even have dances sometimes, since there are nurses and Red Cross workers over there, too. He assures Caroline that he stays firmly in his seat. And he promises her a dance the minute he returns.

October 24

The days pass by slowly and I hardly write now because there is simply nothing to write about. I worry about Will every day, as we haven't heard from him in weeks. This is how I spend my time — worrying and feeling anxious and worrying some more. Although I have gone back to volunteering for the YMCA, I do not feel useful at all. I feel perfectly useless.

November 2

Each day I wait for something to happen. Some new something to happen. And each night, I come to my room, change into my nightclothes, and sigh. I am terribly frustrated indeed. We went to war more than six months ago now, and all I can do is sit here and read while the rest of the world (and Will) fight for me. Unfair, I say.

November 10

I am uncertain of my feelings toward this Women's Peace Party. Of course, I am very much in favor of peace. But I am as much in favor of defending ourselves and our country. I do think these women quite something, though, for they are very hard at work trying for women's suffrage as well. Of that, I am very much in favor! Something good might come from war after all.

Francie has joined the ranks of the suffragists and I'm quite sure her mother has finally given up! Francie isn't allowed to picket or anything since she is too young, but she manages to stay pretty informed and pretty close to the action downtown. She agrees with me that we ought to defend ourselves in this war. She just thinks President Wilson ought to settle some internal wars here on the home front, too. She's becoming a rather knowledgeable person — and she's even more fascinating for it! I'm glad to have her around now more than ever.

November 13

What a glorious day! The sun is shining, the air is crisp, and I have a plan. Today, General John J. Pershing himself called for young women to join his ranks. It said so in the newspaper. And, I am ready to report.

Pershing has put AT&T in charge of selecting and

then training French-speaking American girls to operate the switchboards on the Western Front. At present, I am plotting my way into the Signal Corps. Oui, moi!

November 15

I am so mad I could scream. I did scream. I actually climbed the staircase taking two stairs at once, threw off my cape at the top, and pulled my bedroom door closed with more force than I knew I had. And then I let out a noise that I think has been building inside of me for years. Years of being perfectly dressed, perfectly groomed, perfectly educated, perfectly bored! Then, this marvelous gift presents itself, and now it is gone.

More later. I must go retrieve my cape.

Later

They told me I was much too young to join up. I lied to Maman about where I was going, walked all the way to the Armory, presented myself enthusiastically (but without a curtsy, as I believe that might have indicated too feminine an inclination for army work) — and they told me I was simply too young but thank you very much for your patriotism. Hmmmph. And there I thought Maman's insistence on speaking French in the house might finally pay off.

Will and I still joke about "France for a day." That's what Maman called it. Go to sleep one night in New York City. Wake up the very next day and you are in Paris. It was an indulgence we allowed her, but we felt silly most of the time. We'd sit at an imaginary café and Maman would play a waitress who understood only French (she loved playing the role). It was a bit frustrating. No English allowed. Maman's rules. Merveilleux. I know French but have no use for it. I must sleep now.

November 20

I have finished *The House of Mirth* by Edith Wharton and am grief-stricken. I had hoped Lily Bart would find herself stronger in the end. I had hoped that she would have found her way to independence. The story takes place mostly in this very neighborhood just about the time when Maman moved into Father's house. Things have changed, if only slightly from then, though. I grant that this society of ours is still stifling, but I think a woman holds more power nowadays. Why, I could go right out and get myself a job today. I met a girl recently who works at a flower shop and lives at a boarding house all by herself. She is my age! Perhaps she doesn't use fine silver to dine or wear the newest fashions, but she certainly seemed content to me.

Miss Wharton grew up right here in New York City, a society girl. She lives in Paris now. She gave all this up to go on an adventure. She is no Lily Bart and neither shall I be.

November 23

Thanksgiving indeed! The age requirement for the Army Signal Corps has been lifted and the training age as well. They hadn't realized how few girls speak French well enough to communicate with ease. Well, merci, Maman!

P.S. Finally, another letter from Will. He is all right. He was writing while on a day leave in Paris. I wonder if he'll run into Ms. Wharton. Perhaps I will . . .

November 25

I was only a little surprised when Maman reacted so calmly to my announcement, especially considering how much I've been stomping around this house like a child. I thought she might decide to treat me like one, when I finally told them my plans last night.

I actually had to steady myself in my chair at the dining room table by grasping my seat from underneath. In a way, I was holding on as much in preparation for my own reaction as I was for theirs. Once I said it aloud, it would be official. I would have to go through with it.

In my head I had rehearsed several hundred times what I would say. Finally, I blurted it out. "I've volunteered to go overseas to France with the armed forces." Father, who had until that moment been merely pondering his plate, paused for a moment, then looked deeper into his mashed potatoes. Staring, I presume, to avoid the reality of my words. I was leaving home to go to war.

When I explained further, when I told them that I was to be part of the Army Signal Corps, when I told them all about how I would train right here in the city first, then be shipped out there to help our soldiers (our Will) communicate from the trenches, Maman simply sighed. "I imagine there is hardly more danger for a switchboard operator over there than there is right here in the city on any given night." Silence. Then, slowly (slyly actually), her eyebrows relaxed and her lips unpursed and broke into a wide smile. That was that! As I had hoped, she was proud.

Then, finally, Father put down his fork and looked at me. Do you know what he said? "Well, you must make sure and visit the old bakeshop in Paris." Oh, I was so relieved. At last, I could share my excitement and start preparing.

December 1

A letter from Thomas! He has indeed gone to California and already has a job working on the set of a movie. What a dream. He made a big deal of apologizing for not saying good-bye before he left. He did say that he made sure to write his parents this time. He said he was afraid to see anyone before he left. He thought he might not go if he felt like he had any ties to New York. Then he wrote this, "When there's nothing to keep you tied to home, there's nothing to keep you from living your dreams."

Now that's something. Here I thought that without any ties to anyone or anyplace, I wouldn't feel brave enough to do anything at all in this world. But Thomas, he feels just the opposite way. He feels braver for it. Well, I bet that deep down he's very glad to have his parents know just where he is. I'd make a big bet on that.

December 5

I got my telegram today! It came from the Office of the Chief Signal Officer. It's official now. I must be sworn in all on my own by a notary public or by a justice of the peace . . . "as required under the provisions of the Articles of War and Army regulations"! Can you imagine? Moi? An officer in the United States Army.

December 10

It happens that a friend of Father's is a justice of the peace, so Maman is going to throw a little party here at the house for after I take my oath tonight! More later. Francie is on her way over.

Later

I am officially a member of the U.S. Army! The oath took but a minute, and now I'm really going. It's really going to happen.

The Grandparents were here and I think that in spite of themselves, they were proud of me. The Walkers came over, too — Francie and her parents. Mrs. Walker gave Maman an awfully hard time about my going off to the war. She said that this was the most inappropriate time for me to be leaving, as this is when I would be most likely to find a husband. Francie, of course, stood behind her mother while she talked and rolled her eyes very dramatically, which made it hard not to laugh.

But Maman and I had such a laugh when we talked about it after she left. Here we thought she was upset that I was going to be in danger or something. But, no! She was just worried I wouldn't find a husband! We decided that I'll be meeting all kinds of interesting people over there. And Maman asked, "Won't it be much more romantic to find yourself in France than to find yourself a husband?" Oui, Maman, I do believe it would!

December 15

I'm looking forward to Christmas, but worried about the fact that the war isn't nearing the end. Will seemed so sure that he'd be home for Christmas. And I haven't even gone yet. They must think there is still a lot of warring to do if they still want me to train and go over there.

December 16

What a wonderful day I had. Maman took Francie and me to the most marvelous shop so that we could get some Christmas spirit in us, she said. Enough gloominess, we all agreed.

The shop itself was like Christmas in a box! The whole place smelled like the inside of a fireplace and little pine trees were decorated with ornaments of all kinds. There were lovely crystals in the shape of icicles, carved wooden Santas and sleighs, and little balls of silver and gold everywhere. But what caught my eye was the most special of all — it was an angel made of porcelain. Her face was so detailed and the feel of her so smooth, that tears filled my eyes.

Well, Maman was already paying the clerk for her basket full of Christmas so I thought I'd leave the angel where she was, and off we went to the bakery where Maman treated us to gingersnap cookies and hot chocolate. By the time we got home, dark was setting in and our breath made puffs of white in the night air. Inside, a fire in the fireplace warmed us and Maman's plan had worked. It is beginning to feel like Christmas.

December 24

We stayed up until now (11:30!) decorating the tree and playing "Ask Me Another." What fun! I adore thinking games. Maman always thinks more creatively than Father and me. She actually chose the Kaiser as her subject! I'm afraid Father and I didn't come close — we asked question after question and yet we ended up guessing President Wilson. How interesting that we could mix up the two like that. One is so good and one so dangerous. But, without knowing the details of their lives, one leader seems just like another.

And so, it is just about Christmas and I miss Will. Caroline is coming over to spend the day with us. She actually told Maman that being with us makes her feel closer to Will. I think I like her more than ever.

December 25

Christmas! Father and Maman gave me the gift of my army uniform. We were responsible for purchasing them on our own, and they are quite expensive. I am fortunate that we can afford it so easily. It is really quite chic — a lovely dark blue wool Norfolk jacket paired with a matching long skirt and a fashionable wide-brimmed hat, which Maman might as well have made herself, it is so nice. The sad part is that we must wear hideous sateen bloomers underneath in case our skirts should be blown up in the wind!

So, I tried it on immediately and modeled for everyone. When I made my final turn, I saw Sally standing in the doorway of the parlor with tears in her eyes. The tray of brandies she was holding started to rattle. Maman hurried over to her and took the tray. Sally sat with us and the room got quiet. "First William, and now Simone," she said. The air was so heavy that I thought I might cry, too. But Maman didn't miss a step. She passed around the brandies and raised her glass. "When Christmas comes again, we shall all be together . . . and the world will be a safer place."

Now I sit here remembering that Will said just those

words when he left that day. So I wonder, if he thought the war would be over by this Christmas, and if the war is still going so strong that they are sending dozens more soldiers (and nurses) all the time, what makes everyone so sure that when Christmas comes again, we will be any closer to victory?

December 31

New Year's Eve. We are off to dinner at the Oak Room at the Plaza. How divine!

Later, January 1, 1918

I suppose it isn't just "later," but a whole new year for the world and for me. I am eighteen years old now. Many times in my life, people have noted that I will always know how old I am by the year, for I was born on the first day of the new century. Maman said to me today that being born amid so much change is what makes me an adventurous soul, born without the restrictions of the last century upon me. Born into a new time for women and for the world. She says something similar every year.

Sometimes I think of it that way, but mostly, I feel

lucky that each year my birthday falls on the first day of a new year. This is very inspiring to me.

Anyway, we have just come home from the very lovely restaurant inside the Plaza (which is perhaps the most exceptional place I've been so far in my life), and seeing as I ushered in this new dawn by stuffing myself silly, I think I better give up for tonight and start fresh tomorrow!

January 12

It is very early in the morning and I am writing simply to record the day my service in the army began. I am off to training day number one. I can hardly imagine that operating a switchboard is terribly difficult.

Later

I just re-read what I wrote so early this morning. If only I had been right. This is not easy at all. I think being a nurse might have been easier! Well, different anyway. There are so many things to remember, so many codes and exchanges. A woman named Grace Banker has been put in charge of us — she is chief operator. She once worked as an instructress for AT&T and is now a graduate of Barnard College right here in New York City.

From what I was told, our work overseas will be harder still, for we will be operating under the stress of war. We will have to make translations and act quickly to relay the proper messages to our soldiers. I suppose I will just have to work very hard between now and then to make sure I make no mistakes. I will not risk the life of a soldier.

I admit that Will being over there motivates me somewhat. Will he be among the soldiers I communicate with over the telephone lines? Will I see him face to face?

January 20

The other girls, or women, rather, are not happy about my being part of their group. They are mostly staying at boarding houses while we complete training and then await our ship to Europe. I am self-conscious now about where I come from. I've taken to walking to the training center each day since I heard some nasty comments about my being dropped off by Max that first day. (Father still insists that Max pick me up in the evenings.)

Most of the girls seem to come from very modest

places indeed. One girl even came here all the way from North Dakota. Cordelia is her name. She is one of seventeen children! They all live together on a prairie farm. (I picture her as Mary Pickford was in *Rebecca of Sunnybrook Farm!*) This is her first time in New York City. I think I would never have been brave enough to come all the way here (let alone to France) if I ever knew only North Dakota. But she seems even more confident than I am. I am clearly the youngest at eighteen, though I feel more like a twelve year old around these girls. Perhaps growing up in this city hasn't prepared me as much as I thought it had. I truly believed that I would have an advantage, living here all my life. I am beginning to realize, though, that I have not encountered very much in my time.

Oh, I hear about the goings on in the city. I've read the papers since the moment I could read at all, and I've listened at the door of Father's study since I was a little girl. But I have not ever had to do anything on my own. It is easy to feel superior when you have a man to drive you around all day, or when you have all the dresses and hats a girl could ever want. It is easy to feel that way until you meet a girl nearly your very own age who has milked cows, diapered babies, and gotten up morning after morning to cook for her family since the age of six!

I like Cordelia very much, though. She is the only one who even considers me. Every morning she greets me when the others roll their eyes. And today, she said the most intriguing thing. When I asked her if she could believe that they were actually going to let us girls get so close to the front lines, she simply said, "I can believe it all right. I just can't believe you think of us as girls. We are women, Simone." When I think of a woman, I think of Maman and her friends, or older women with lines on their faces and some gray in their hair, or those women who picket downtown for the vote. They are women. But, us? Perhaps Cordelia and the others. Not me, though. Not yet.

January 25

Not much to write. Each night I come home and collapse. We actually do a daily military drill so that we will be good little soldiers over there. I haven't seen Francie in weeks, between my training and her women's party work. I hope we have some time together before I go. Must sleep now.

February 10

We were sworn in today — some of us for the second time now. When the others went off to a restaurant nearby to celebrate the end of training, I simply lagged behind to spare myself the embarrassment of not being asked to join them. Even Cordelia overlooked me today.

I'm learning that it doesn't matter if you have money or not. It merely matters whether or not you are in the majority.

February 15

Although we are on a bit of a break while we wait for our transport to arrive, we must wear our uniform always. And do you know that because we will be so close to the front lines, and because we are under the same strict military code of conduct as our male counterparts, that we are also subject to court-martial?

Francie and I were absolutely beside ourselves imagining how she would fare under strict military rules. I guess that's why she's taken to marching with the suffragists rather than get involved directly with the war effort. That way she gets to break rules.

February 20

One week until I'm off to war! One week to spend with Maman and Father and Francie without training to break up the day.

February 28

I can't believe the time has come. I am all packed and ready to go. Father went out and got me all of the things they said I will need, like an overcoat, a rubber raincoat, and a pair of brown army boots. I managed to get some personal items in my suitcase as well, including a hairbrush and mirror, and a picture of the whole family from Will's wedding that I'll put next to my bed. Will I even have a bed? Well, I'll put it somewhere close by.

All of a sudden I'm leaving home for the first time in my life — and not even to college, but to war.

More tomorrow . . . when we set sail!

March 1

Here I sit waiting for Maman and Father to take me to
the waterfront. Francie's coming along, too. I'm so excited. Now I don't feel nervous at all. And really, a
switchboard operator's nerves needn't be nearly as steely
as a soldier's.

March 2

Yesterday was such a whirlwind as I said my good-byes
and then got used to this ship (and the sea beneath me),
that when I finally had a moment to myself, I simply
slept. Saying good-bye to Maman proved especially difficult. With Will having departed, I was sure our next
good-bye would be easier. I was terribly wrong.

Also, Francie gave me a gift to take along that pulled
my heart straight out of my chest! She handed me a little red velvet pouch. In it was the angel from the Christmas shop. Francie said, "I saw you admiring it that day
and I thought you should have it with you over there.
Just make sure you bring it back in time to hang on your
tree for Christmas." Well, I just couldn't believe it. Here
it is months from last Christmas, and so many months

to go until the next one, and Francie managed to make it Christmas anyway.

It is lonely on this ship and I'm glad to have the angel with me. But I'm more glad for a friend like Francie.

March 7

I can hardly find the time to write now. I will try to get something down while there is still some light. We sail under the strangest of circumstances. The ship's portholes are covered with "blackout" curtains so that we can travel undetected by German submarines.

The ship itself was converted to a troopship from an ocean liner. To think that this was once a ship filled with people in fine clothes, dining at sunset, a string quartet playing to set their trip to music. Actually, it's not all that different now. We are on this ship with thousands of troops. Us girls, plus more American boys in uniform than you can imagine. We all must wear life jackets, which is just about the only way you'd know there was any danger. Instead, some of the girls have found their way into the soldiers' hearts and they dance and have a gay old time each night. It's fun to watch, but I have kept mostly to myself. I'm feeling a bit shy and overwhelmed.

It was beginning to feel rather real . . . rather exciting, too. But then the drills started. Lifeboat drills, in case we are hit?

To think that I am on the very kind of adventure we so often imagined in the kitchen!

March 9

Things are as usual here on this big boat in the middle of this big ocean. I am so seasick that I think I must have lost several pounds by now. Still, I march into that dining room three times a day and sit with the others at a table just for Signal Corps girls and try not to be sick at the table. Matters are made very much worse due to the soap they insist we use. They have gone to great lengths to promote Lifebuoy Health Soap's effectiveness at combating what the company calls "B.O." (Bad Odor). Well the smell of that soap is so strong it has created a much worse smell than B.O.! I for one wish they'd toss the whole supply into the ocean!

March 15

We have been sleeping in our clothes for days now. We are stuck on a sandbar, and they fear the ship is offering a big, unmoving target for the Germans. There is nothing we can do except to follow orders — orders that are more strict than they have been so far.

March 21

We have been in Southampton (England!) nearly a week now. We must stay here for a bit until we adjust to war rations. I was never a very big eater (and certainly not recently). Well, actually I am a big eater of sweets, could eat them all the day and night. But I've never been terribly interested in the rest of it. Now, I must admit that I'm feeling a bit weak and a lot tired.

I haven't slept very much. The other night when we were still on the water, I went onto the lower deck for some air when I heard noises that sounded like they were coming from a wounded animal. I looked around until a boot sticking out from under a lifeboat caught my eye. I walked over and bent down only to find a girl crying — sobbing, actually. When I asked her what the matter was (I thought she might be ill), she tried to shoo me away. Well, I could not leave her. So, I crawled right under there with her. We just lay there for a short while, when finally I asked her if she was scared. She turned to me and nodded. She said, "Please don't tell the others. They are all being so brave, and here I am crying like a baby, wishing I could turn back." I promised I wouldn't tell a soul.

Then I told her a secret of my own. "I cry in my bed every single night." I haven't even written these words right here, have I? But it's true. And you know what? I would believe it if I found out each and every one of these girls did the same. And some of the boys, too. The girl's name is Alice. I dare say that I've finally made a friend.

March 22

We are en route from Southampton to Le Havre (France!) and with all that has gone wrong, I cannot wait to set foot on land. We have been transferred onto a hospital ship that will get us across the English Channel to France. We must still sleep in our clothes which, according to some officers, is a very necessary plan indeed. They told us of several instances where ships making this very crossing were torpedoed in the middle of the night! (Better to be fully dressed, I suppose, if you're going to be flailing about in the ocean.)

So, imagine my state when Alice and I were on deck today trying to see what we could see through all the fog, and a loud horn blew, nearly knocking us over. There was such a dense fog that we first ran into a submarine net, and then we were nearly hit by another cruiser — a French cruiser. Here I have been worried sick that a German ship would somehow find us. That is what they trained us to worry about after all!

March 23

I think Alice and I will be great friends. She is from Boston, which I think is just a wonderful town. But Alice comes from a very poor family with six children — and she the only girl! Her parents came to America from Ireland (just like Sally) and the way she describes them sounds like something from a storybook. She misses them terribly, the poor girl. We'll be family for now, I told her. I must write to Sally and tell her I've made a new friend she'd surely like to meet.

March 24

I can hardly believe that I am here! Paris! After a train ride that promptly introduced us to the loud noises of war, we have arrived. On that train, we could hear the guns and even a bomb that let us know that the war is no longer an ocean away. It is right here, all around us. We are on the move so I don't have time to write. I simply had to put this moment down. I made it. More later. Much more, I'm sure!

Later (about four in the morning)

The morning I left, Maman and I shared a moment alone and she gave me a short talk about going out into the world. She kept it very brief. (Maman is not one for drawn-out moments.) But she gave me something else that morning. It was a letter. She asked me not to open it until I had arrived safely in Paris. I've opened it now and am moved to tears.

Ma coeur,

*Bienvenue à Paris! I hope now you will truly hear what
French can sound like when it is spoken on a cool spring
morning by the man who sells bread on the Champs-Élysées
as you pass him by. Bon matin, mademoiselle! That is what
he will say, I am sure. And now, you will see the sights of a
new city, ma chérie. Le Louvre, La Tour d'Eiffel, l'arc de
Triomphe! And do you know something else, ma chérie? You
will taste café au lait as it is meant to be. At last you will
see where my love affair began.*

*This brings me to the reason for this letter. I had hoped
you would one day visit my home and that I would be with
you. Although I am sad for the circumstances that brought
you there, I am very proud of you. I am not sure I would
have done the same. I am not sure how my children became
so brave. I have included here a map of Paris from when I
was just about your age. In fact, it is the map Father was
reading the day he walked into the pâtisserie. It is yours
now. Go and see the shop. Go and see my little house at 23
rue d'Orsel, and picture me there, looking out the window
upstairs, wishing on the stars each night. I was wishing for
the very life I now have, you know.*

*Then, I would like for you to do something for me. I
would like for you to go to the graveyard where your*

Grand'mère and Grand'père are buried. I have never been back in all these years. Please bring some tulips and tell them all our news and give them love for me.

You will see that I've circled all of these places. Bonne chance finding them! Be safe, ma coeur.

Je t'aime,
Maman

My eyes are burning. I will write in the morning.

March 25, Early morning

Alice has agreed to join me and help me figure out all of these crooked streets! I know Boston is full of them so she ought to be a better navigator than I. We had to tell our YWCA hostess where we were headed. In each city, there will be a hostess who is responsible for getting our accommodations and anything else we might need. It is exhilarating to me that the YWCA is here just to meet the needs of women war workers, just like the YMCA does for the soldiers! Miss Banker went over all the rules with us, including that we are not to visit any navy or army barracks, nor are we to visit the docks, and that we must let our hostess know where we are going in our free time.

I believe we will not be here too long before they send us all in different directions, so we must get to everything this day!

Later

What a special day it turned out to be. I do believe Alice and I have walked this entire city! First, we did just what Maman said — we walked along the Champs-Élysées and took in the city just before it woke up. Then we sat and had café au lait in the sweetest, tiniest café I could have imagined. Alice was quite impressed with my French. She learned hers in school, and although she speaks correctly (and perhaps her vocabulary is a tad more extensive than mine), well, I have the accent of a native — Maman! Indeed, it is a language only to be spoken like a native. I would never say as much to Alice, though, for perfect accent or not, it is only her ability to speak and understand the language that will matter once we're working those lines. Then we went in search of Maman's house. After winding up and down several wrong streets, we found the little bitty thing.

I cannot believe that my Maman grew up in that house. To think that she is always wishing we had even more space in ours, with all of its rooms and floors. Well, we rang the bell and a very fine older woman was kind enough to let us roam around a bit once I explained that my Maman had grown up there. I went right up to what I knew to be her room and I looked out her window. I felt very close to her just then. I must write to her later.

So, we thanked the lady and she directed us to the cemetery, which we found handily (not before stopping by a florist for some tulips per Maman's request). It was very overgrown and at first I was upset that no one was keeping the place up, but Alice stopped me and said, "Look at it for a minute, Simone. It's very unruly, but that's what makes it so beautiful and natural. It is as it should be, I think. It's romantic." I frowned for a minute. Alice hadn't struck me as a romantic until that moment. But I looked around and found that she was right. It was something wild and beautiful indeed. We had to navigate a lot of prickly weeds in order to get to the headstones, but when we finally found them, it was worth it. There they were: *Jeanette and Christian Mercier.*

Mercier is my middle name. Maman, an only child, could not bear to lose it. I will pass it on for her myself.

On the way back we had one more thing to do — the pâtisserie. But we walked around and around the block where Maman said we'd find it and all we saw was an empty storefront. I fear the most recent owners went out of business. I went to the door and peered inside. I saw the counter where Maman sat that day guarding all of her baked goods when Father walked into her life. I arched my head up trying to see what was above the door. There it was — the bell that rang each time a new customer walked in. Alice and I shook the door a bit until we got the bell to ring the faintest jingle. No matter that I couldn't go inside. The store has been alive for me all my life. Being there today, hearing that little bell, well, it just brought me closer to where I come from.

We finally got back to the hotel in time for a late dinner with all the others. It was a perfect day in Paris.

March 27

Our hotel was nearly hit by an aerial shell last night! The French staff rushed all of us down to the cellar when they heard the noise. Alice came to my room to make sure I was all right and together we ran down five flights of stairs — some of the girls even slid down the banisters in their nightgowns! It was rather funny at the time — the chaos. I mean such a serious bunch of girls sliding down the railing in nightgowns? It makes me chuckle even now.

Of course we woke up this morning to find a hole in the ground where the building next to ours used to be. I wasn't laughing then.

March 28

Alice and I were thrilled to find out that we are going to be stationed together! We are going to Chaumont sur Haute-Marne with about ten other girls. Another group went to a town called Tours, and still others will stay here in Paris. I'm happy to be off to Chaumont — it is where the advanced section of General Pershing's American Expeditionary Forces is headquartered. How exciting! (Scary, too!)

April 5

Again, the YWCA has arranged for our housing. For now we are each living with a French family. My hosts (the names of whom I forgot the moment they were told to me) seem very hospitable. I'm sure they're not terribly pleased with me as I can't be very social with them — we must start working right away in the morning. And I must sleep. Will I remember their names in the morning? Perhaps I won't need to — this place is so small, I don't imagine there will be much shouting of names from faraway rooms!

I think Alice is staying with another family nearby. It has been a long day with even more changes and I am tired.

April 6

Well, I am completely in love with this town. I always thought that I was one hundred percent a city girl. Even though I always liked spending time in Newport, I didn't find it to be terribly different from the city itself. I suppose the air there is a little fresher and the scenery greener and much more open. But, this! The view opens up into forever. Chaumont is set up on a hilltop, overlooking the valleys of the Suize and Marne rivers. Flowers cover the countryside and the air smells better than any I have ever breathed.

This afternoon, after we completed our first shift at the office, Alice and I went exploring a bit and found a wonderful château. As it turns out, it is where General Pershing, our commander in chief, is in residence! It makes me feel very close to the action.

The work is confusing and I was worried I'd make a mistake right away. Luckily, we spent more time getting acquainted with the office than we did in managing calls. I did handle a few calls, though, and the nicest thing happened. I picked up a call on a line of the local switchboard and said, "Number, please," in English to a soldier wishing to put a call through. Well, he practically jumped through the wire he was so thrilled to hear an American voice pick up. "Thank heaven you're here at last!" he yelled over and over. Perhaps General Pershing had something else in mind besides wanting bilingual operators to be able to communicate with both French and American soldiers. Perhaps he thought hearing a nice American girl's voice on the line just might lift the spirits of our doughboys. At any rate, it's a benefit even if Pershing didn't think of it, and I'm proud as can be to be here for them.

I must get to sleep. The words are blurring as I write them.

April 16

I can't believe how difficult it is to write regularly. We are still living out of our suitcases. Every day we work for ten hours at the switchboard and then we must come home and cook dinner. The work is exhausting, too. I see I haven't written in more than a week. With all the commotion, I find myself without even an ounce of energy left to pick up my pen at the end of each day. But tonight I must write for just a minute before I lose track of where I am!

The U.S. telephone office is located in a small room on the first floor of the army barracks. We moved in that first day and got to work. Up until that point, male operators had been working the lines. I must say, they didn't seem too keen on us girls walking in and taking the place over. I think it's quite something that we're here, too. But I am confident that we will do our job well. The other day I heard someone talking about how they had to start replacing some of the male army office workers with women so that the men could fight. They were concerned that it would take two women to do the job of just one man. Only, they discovered that in fact, two women were able to do the work of three men and in less time! Ha!

The soldiers are calling us "hello girls" for the nice way we pick up their calls. I'll make sure to say some extra cheerful "hellos" tomorrow.

April 26

I realize I'm writing even less now. I think it's because of the routine. Every day it's the same thing, sitting at that switchboard, handling all of the calls that come in and out, trying hard not to make any mistakes. I try not to think too much and just let myself do what I've been trained to do. I'm learning to trust myself. But, it has been incredibly noisy, which doesn't make anything easier.

The exchange, where all of the switchboards are located, has to be enlarged. We have to work straight through while they work around us. My head hurts from concentrating so hard.

For the moment, many of the calls have to be routed through the local French lines. Their exchange is handled by French women in the civil service. They sit in the rear of our office and are somewhat unhelpful. I will say that the very relaxed way of life, which is so evident in this lovely countryside, is also evident in the way these women handle their calls and our questions! (Now I know why those boys were so relieved to hear our voices on the lines in those first days.) I'm not sure they know there is a war going on the way they take their time getting us the information we need. Perhaps they just don't understand the kind of difference that even a few seconds delay might make. I know the soldiers do, for every time we meet a soldier on the lines, they give us the town codes without pause.

I hope we will move into our new living quarters soon. The days are so long — it would be nice if we could all go home to the same place and share the day's trials. I don't mean to complain. I came here to work hard. And my host family has indeed been kind. (Whatever their names may be!) And I do consider this a privilege, a chance to do whatever I can to help win this war. I just want to feel less lonely doing it.

May 5

At last we are living better. We have been moved into the most marvelous stone house. It even has a bathtub! We are so proud of that. I can't even remember the last time I felt clean. So many homes around here are without bathtubs that I realize now how very fortunate I was in my upbringing. I never could have imagined going without a bath at home. And now it has been, what? Weeks, I think! Oh well, I am delighted to get a little cleaner now.

The best part of this house is that we all come home to one another, which makes everything more bearable. Mostly, Alice and I are on the same work schedule so we spend our off time together talking about anything we can think of that has nothing to do with war. She tells me about the Kealy family and I tell her about mine, along with Francie and Sally, too.

May 12

The routine continues. At least they have put in more American phone lines so that work is easier and we do have a bit more time to relax, if only for an hour. There are two types of switchboards that we work — one is used for ordinary local and long-distance calls, usually having to do with supplies and transportations, and one that carries all of the messages between fighting units and their commanding officers who direct the troops' every movement. We call these the fighting lines since every order for an infantry advance or some kind of troop movement comes in through them. For now, I stick to the ordinary switchboard, but soon I know I will be able to handle the whole exchange.

I do feel far away from the action still, but today a long-distance call came in from an officer who needed to order equipment. I could hear the guns in the background! I quickly connected him and felt some satisfaction at being there for him right then.

May 20

Alice and I went for a walk out in the valley this evening. We were so pleased the sun decided to stay just a few moments longer because everything looked just beautiful in the orange and purple light. We even got a chance to smell the violets, which I had thought gone by now. And the lilies of the valley seem to be overtaking the whole place. I have plucked a few and stuck them in the envelope with my weekly letter to Maman. They're her favorite. She would love a place where they grow wild.

May 25

American doughboys seem to have taken over this town. They are all beginning to look the same. But I search the sea of faces anyhow, just in case one of them might be Will.

We are taken to work each day in a car driven by officers who are very kind to us. We have made friends with them on all those rides to and from the exchange.

There is going to be a dance for us next week, which will be nice. We are all so worn out all the time, but a bit bored, too, I dare say. Some of the girls have their eyes on particular boys with whom they're hoping to have a dance.

June 1

I still can't believe this night. I saw Will! Oh, the whole thing could have been pulled straight from the movies. I'd like to start with the best part, but I want to write about the night from start to finish so that I will always remember it. Plus, I plan to write home tomorrow and tell Maman every detail, so this will help!

There was a dance tonight that we were all rather excited about since things are a bit dull around here. I must say that I thought every single day would be an adventure and the truth of it is that some days, I might as well be back in New York City. So, we were all giggles getting ready for this dance. We had to wear our uniforms, of course, so there wasn't much we could do to make ourselves look special. There is something about wearing this uniform that is freeing in that way. At home, I must be so very aware of my appearance. Just to walk out the door, I must be dressed, really dressed. I don't think I realized just how difficult that was — to be so scrutinized all the time.

So, instead of trying on new dresses, we tried on some makeup! Oh, just a very little bit, but it was fun anyhow. And then we curled our hair up so it fell in little ringlets just like Mary Pickford herself! We were having such a ball, I actually thought that getting ready would prove to be the best part of the night. It often is, you know.

We all walked over to the dance since it was just around the block. Alice put her arm in mine as we walked and I was reminded of Maman. She always walks like that. It is a very happy way to walk around. That's how we all felt tonight. Alive and happy. So, we walked in to the dance hall and they had decorated it and everything. It was exciting. Especially because the soldiers were there already. They had been there for a bit from the looks of things. They were hanging around in their seats looking awfully bored and a bit anxious, too.

Alice squeezed my hand. She's a bit crazier for the boys than I am. She was already pointing one of them out when I spotted him. He was laughing and his eyes were all crinkled up just like always. My eyes welled up so much that the tears clogged my throat and I could not speak. It was Will.

Alice was tugging on my arm, demanding to know what was the matter. Then, he saw me, too! Thank goodness, because he came right over and picked me up off my feet and suddenly the shock wore off. I hugged him so hard. I mean I knew he was all right because we hadn't heard otherwise, but to see him — well, it's been so long. I didn't know how much I had been missing him.

The thing is, he was in shock, too. Maman never wrote to him that I was coming over because she thought it might upset or distract him. He was practically shaking me as he yelled questions at me. What was I doing there? Why was I in uniform? He was out of his mind! We both calmed down long enough to make some introductions. I must admit that I was so proud of my brother in his uniform that I wanted each and every girl to meet him and know he was my brother. They all know by now that he's married of course, so most of them were rather obvious about looking over his shoulder at his friends!

We finally sat down together at a small table in the corner and we talked about everything. He knew a lot already from my letters. But he didn't know that I had joined the army. I told him all about training and the trip over here. He said that he heard about Pershing making the call for bilingual telephone operators. He said he even thought of me, but he had assumed I wouldn't meet the age requirement. He also admitted that he thought it would be dangerous, and so he decided not to mention it to me. Well, lucky for me, I found out about it all on my own.

He hasn't seen too much action yet, he said. They have mostly been around here waiting in the wings, I suppose for something to happen. Deep in my heart somewhere, I was so relieved to hear that. I could tell, though, that it disappointed him somewhat, and I understood completely. After all, we're here to do something. Both of us.

Even if that were all that happened tonight, it would surely be enough. But, there's one thing more. As Will and I sat there, a young man came toward us and for some reason, my heart pounded right away.

He didn't even say a word to Will. He just stuck his hand out and said, "Sam." Well, I gave him my hand and shook it extra hard (so he wouldn't know I was thrown) and I looked at Will with big eyes, hoping he would step in. He hit Sam in the arm and said, "Sam, this is my younger sister, Simone. And she is an officer in the army." Then he said, "Simone, this is Sam Cates." The introduction gave me a moment to compose myself at least. Although, I had to be reminded of his last name later, since I really wasn't listening when Will said it. I was busy looking at Sam whatever his last name was.

He is tall and strong. Not bulky like an athlete, but strong nevertheless. I could tell because his uniform fit perfectly on his shoulders. The other boys have a little trouble filling in those broad-shouldered uniforms. But, you know, it was not even his handsome looks that stopped me so. I believe it was something else. You see, I've met lots of boys before. All the parties back in school, and certainly at the summer parties in the country. Of course, I've been around boys. And they've liked me, some of them. But until this moment I never did feel anything but a fondness for any of them.

Mostly the boys I know from home are well bred, very bright, and polite, too. Perhaps it was Maman filling my head (and my heart) with stories of true love, or maybe it was that one in particular. The one where she and Father simply stopped the world turning when they met. Whatever the reason, I never could be bothered with any boy that did not stop my world. But Sam. He stopped it indeed.

We sat there all night after that. My girlfriends came over and joined us, and some of the other boys did the same. They told us stories that made us laugh. Alice even laughed some punch right out of her nose! And at that moment, I thought of Francie. She would have laughed just the same way, and all the boys would have been just as charmed.

Well it all had to end, of course, since it was well past our curfew. We all said some polite good-byes and Will promised to come by tomorrow and stay in close touch until his assignment changed. I thought Sam might let me go without saying a word, and I deflated a bit. But then, he touched my arm on the way out and said, "Next time, we should actually dance, don't you think?" The others pulled him away and I didn't get to answer.

Now, I am here with my hand all cramped up so I must stop writing and try with all my might to get some sleep. I hope I wake up with my head on straight again. Falling in love wouldn't be at all convenient right now.

June 2

Will came by today during my shift break, but I am sad to report that Sam was not with him. I did not say a word to Will about it, hoping all the while that *he* would. But he left after we shared a coffee and a letter he received from Caroline.

Well, back on track, I say! I'm sure he would have paid me a call if this were to be the love of my life. Father offered to buy every pastry in the shop, didn't he? Sam could have at least paid a call.

June 6

That Sam Cates is something else. If I tell you that I have never in my life met a more incorrigible man, well, it would be no exaggeration at all. I think I know what I found so charming about him that first night — he barely spoke a word! Oh sure, it is very easy to like a person a whole lot when he stands in front of you and stares you down in his uniform looking handsome and brave as can be. Too easy, for I know now that handsome is all he is, plus mean. Add that he has no manners at all and is all too full of himself, and you understand why I never want to see him again.

Tonight, I was so excited when I saw that Sam had come with Will to have dinner with Alice and me, my stomach actually flipped. If only I had known. Perhaps I wouldn't have wasted all those manners on him. All those careful smiles and stupid compliments, too! There I was, oohing and aahing over him and he was doing the same for a while. But then, we started to talk about home. At first, it was a nice, nostalgic conversation. It turns out Sam is from New York also. What luck! Not really.

Because I started to tell them all about Maman's hat shop and then I got all wrapped up in how I believe that New York is the most wonderful city and how Central Park looks so divine all dressed up in the latest fashions. I started to feel a bit self-conscious when Alice and Sam exchanged a look. So, I turned to Will and told him about Juliana's party right after he left and how all the boys were asking after him. Then it happened. (I have to write the whole thing down right here just to stop my mind from playing it over and over.)

"Juliana Gardner?" Sam asked with this very big grin on his face. "Yes," I said, thinking what a coincidence it would be if they happened to know each other. "Do you know her?" "No, Simone," he said suddenly, with a very condescending tone, "I don't know her. I just know of her. I didn't realize that you and Will were part of that set. You both seemed smarter than that." With that, I was taken aback indeed!

Now, let's remember that I am not terribly fond of Juliana, but at that moment I defended her like she was my very best friend in the world. "Why, what do you know of Juliana if you've never even met her?" I snapped at him.

He snapped back. "I know that she is a little rich girl who thinks she is entitled to most anything. I know that she never asks for anything politely and instead orders people around. And now I know that you're friendly with her. I think that's all I need to know." He was look-ing at me with anger, as if I had betrayed him somehow.

As if I had ordered him around. And I was getting angry myself.

"And how do you know all of this, Sam Cates? You haven't yet answered my question. How on earth do you know so much?"

And then with a real sneer he said, "Well, Simone, I suppose I know because my mother worked in her house for her whole life." And there it was.

Will tried to smooth things over. "Ah yes," he said, "the Gardners are something else. I'm not even sure why we continue to associate with them." But I couldn't let him get away with that. Perhaps I should have let Will take over. Perhaps I should have just let Sam be angry with us. But I didn't.

"Just a minute, Will." I said to my brother as I looked directly at Sam. "Say what you will about Juliana, but don't tell me she doesn't treat people well. I've never seen her be even the least bit mean. She wouldn't dare. She's too well bred. That's what I know." Sam put down the glass of beer he had been sipping and looked at me wildly. "Of course that's what you see. Of course she wouldn't be anything but sweet as pie to you and Will and everyone else she thinks worthy. Do you honestly think that's the way she is when the party is over and that big old door on Fifth Avenue closes behind you? Of course that's what you think. Listen to the way you talk about New York, like it's just so marvelous." He was mocking my voice now. "You see the people strutting around the park in their fashionable clothes and your mother's precious hats. You see that clearly. But you don't see too much else do you? Do you know what kind of conditions other people live in, Simone? Do you know what it's like to work in a factory twelve hours a day and then come home to a one-room apartment that you share with five or six other people? And I think you must honestly believe that you are adored by 'the help,' when they laugh at you the moment you leave the room." My eyes were on fire with tears.

"Now, just a minute there, Sam," Will finally stopped him. "We are not the Gardners. Just because we live in a nice house and have the money to pay for help doesn't make us bad people, and it doesn't make us ignorant either. I think you owe Simone an apology." But I wouldn't allow it. I would not allow this silly, angry boy the satisfaction.

"Actually, Will, I think Sam is absolutely correct. After all, whatever his family has suffered in their life, whatever hardship he has endured, well, it must be all my fault." I looked at Alice who had sunk so far into her chair to avoid this scene that I had nearly forgotten she was there. "Alice, I realize you are a much better person than I am, having grown up very poor and on the wrong side of town, but would you do me the favor of walking home with me? I am so spoiled I fear I will not make it by myself. And perhaps I will not even be able to do my job tomorrow. You know, the job where we work twelve-hour days making sure the soldiers in the trenches know what to do next and how to do it?" (Yes, I said all of it, just like that!) And with that, I kissed my brother who was laughing, and Alice and I walked home arm in arm, just like always.

Looking back on the night, I think that I was so happy to find out that Sam was from New York and then so disappointed to find out that he wasn't from the same place as me. I never thought of myself like that. But the way he looked at me differently when he found out where I was from before even knowing a smidge more about me than that, it made me want to look at him differently just so he should know how it feels. The point is, he was mean and I will never waste another smile or belly-flip on Sam Cates — not ever.

June 7

Will came by this afternoon to apologize for his friend's behavior. I told him not to worry, that I hadn't given it another thought.

"But you seemed to like him so much, Simone," Will suggested.

"There's plenty of handsome soldiers here, Will. After a while, they all look the same. Sam's no different, is he?" I replied.

"Actually, I think he is. He likes you, you know? He just didn't realize that we were different from him. And now after thinking it over, he must know that we really aren't. He is embarrassed about where he comes from and he handles it badly. But don't tell me you can't understand that. You and I both know the truth about Juliana Gardner." And then we laughed. He was right.

Will insisted that I go to the dance they're having tonight. He thinks they'll be moving out very soon and wants to have some fun before he goes. I told him I'd think about it.

Later

All the girls are getting ready for the dance and I am sitting here sulking instead. Alice thinks I am being ridiculous. She says that I must care an awful lot about Sam, otherwise I wouldn't let him get to me. Maybe I'll go get ready.

Much, much later!

I am out of breath. I ran all the way back here because walking was just too slow for my reeling mind. I actually tripped and laughed out loud, then covered my mouth, for I could not be discovered out at night, all by myself!

I went to the dance after all and I am still hot in the face from the events of the night. Alice waited for me so we got to the dance late. When we walked in I saw Will right away but didn't see Sam. I was a little disappointed, though I acted relieved to Alice. I think she knew better.

As we walked over to Will, Sam appeared at the table with punch for everyone. "Two more for punch, I see," he said, looking at Alice and me with a smirk. Then he fixed his eyes right on mine and said, "Simone, don't lift a finger. I'll get you yours. I know how delicate you society girls are." He was laughing and I gave serious thought to walking right back out the door at that moment. I changed my mind and replied, "Yes, Sam, will you be a dear and do that?" I had decided to play along. "And, why don't you get Alice and me some chairs while you're at it? What do you mean letting us stand here all this time? I'm already feeling faint." Alice and I burst into hysterics just then and faked fainting spells, our knees fake-buckling under us. There I was down on the floor beside Alice, feeling giddy and silly when Sam came over and took my hand. I looked at him straight in the eyes, defying him to make one more joke about me. "Okay," he said. "Touché." And he pulled me to my feet.

Will came over to help Alice up and then said, "I, for one, think a dance is in order for the two of you — it will seal the peace treaty." Then, as if we were in a movie, the Victrola switched records to one that must have been written for this very war. Sam, who had not yet let go of my hand after helping me up, agreed and guided me to the dance floor and bowed to me as a true gentleman would. We began to dance. Until that moment, I had, in my lifetime, only danced with Father, who makes me dance with him on special occasions and sometimes just in the library for no reason at all, to no music at all. But I had never danced like this.

If I had to guess, I'd think that everyone in the room thought we had danced together before. I fell right into step with him, despite wanting to remain stiff in protest. But as the music played, the voices almost whispering some of the most romantic words I've ever heard, our feet slowed down until we were hardly moving at all. And then we stopped, staring into each other's eyes. I was paralyzed. I was hoping someone would turn up the volume so that my pounding heart would not be audible to the whole room. Instead, the music stopped, and we still didn't move. I remember every word of that song and I will forever.

TILL WE MEET AGAIN
There's a song in the land of the lily,
Each sweetheart has heard with a sigh.
Over high garden walls this sweet echo falls
As a soldier boy whispers good-bye:

Smile the while you kiss me sad adieu
When the clouds roll by I'll come to you.
Then the skies will seem more blue,
Down in Lover's Lane, my dearie.

Wedding bells will ring so merrily
Ev'ry tear will be a memory.
So wait and pray each night for me
Till we meet again.

Tho' good-bye means the birth of a teardrop,
Hello means the birth of a smile.
And the smile will erase the tear blighting trace,
When we meet in the after awhile.

All of the fighting we had done, all of the mad in me, it just went away, and I felt in the deepest down part of me that this was love. This would be my love story.

We danced more after that. Sam made them play that song at least twice more. (This is probably why I remember all the words!) Then, when the others weren't looking, Sam pulled me outside into the night air and we ran away from the hall until we were safely out of sight from the chaperones. I started to yell at him that I could get in very big trouble, but I stopped myself so as not to invite more criticism of my very disciplined life. He smiled at me then and we found a bench where we sat and talked for a good long time. He apologized for being so nasty and I accepted. He started to say that life at 88 Orchard Street (I don't even know where that is!)

wasn't as easy as it was for me growing up. But I hushed him. I told him that we should only talk about good things now. No need to fight with all this fighting going on around us.

The real reason I stopped him is because I didn't want to hear it. When he said those words, he offered a glimpse of himself, a sadness in him, that I hadn't noticed before. Where he was so strong before and so exasperating, he was suddenly fragile. But he spoke so gently that I found myself feeling even more fond of him. There is something very complicated about a boy who can make terrible fun of you, seem in fact to hate you, and then play a love song over and over just for you for the whole rest of the evening. Or maybe it's not complicated at all. Maybe that's just how we resist what love brings. Maybe hating somebody is easier.

Anyway, suddenly I realized that I was out after curfew and I panicked. I got up to go and Sam grabbed my hand. I told him I'd see him tomorrow, but he shook his head. "We're leaving tomorrow, Simone. 'So wait and pray each night for me' just like the song says." At that, I sunk. I couldn't believe I hadn't said good-bye to Will. I didn't even give him the chance to tell me he was moving out.

I reached into my pocket and pulled out the porcelain angel that I have carried with me each and every day since Francie gave it to me. "Take this, Sam. It will watch over you and Will. Tell Will to come home safely. Tell him he's already missed one Christmas so he had better plan to be home for the next one. I'll be there." I turned and almost walked away right then, but I turned back around and blurted out, "And Sam, you come home safely, too. I'll wait and pray. I promise." Then I kissed him right on his lips and ran away from him, ran all the way back to the house!

Alice had waited up. She was so relieved to see me since she had lied to the others that I left the dance early with a stomachache. I told her what happened and now I have written every last detail of it here. For posterity.

June 15

Things are back to normal around here, seeing as my love story is out of my hands for now. We simply work, and the work is a bit strange! We find ourselves doing more than just working the lines. They have enlisted our help in moving foodstuffs around and finding gasoline for the transport officials. I'm somewhat glad to be asked to help out with this kind of work as it breaks up some of the monotony of my days.

July 1

We are off to Neufchâteau now where the First Corps headquarters are located. It will be closer to the front than any girls have gone so far! I don't suppose there will be any monotony there.

July 4

America's Independence Day. I've come a long way from sipping tea on the Lawson's lawn in Newport! Here, Alice and I share a room in real barracks built by the government. There is even a recreation room. The barracks are on the grounds of a house where there is a kitchen and dining room. Our YWCA hostess stays there. I wonder, if I had stayed involved with the Y instead of volunteering for the hospital, if I would be over here working for them, doling out soup and lemonade to soldiers. They do a great deal of good, those girls. They tell the soldiers news about their friends in other squads, they make sure to collect letters for mailing, and they help keep moral nice and high by putting on little shows for everyone with songs and everything.

I wonder now if I would have met Sam if I had come over with the Y. I wonder what would be different and what would be the same.

July 6

Working the switchboards here is an entirely different experience. Our knowledge of French makes us the only link between the advancing American and French units. Our translations have to be rapid and correct. Because the soldiers at either end cannot hear one another, we have to relay actual military messages. We are now living with the constant pressure that a misinterpretation could mean an artillery barrage falling on friendly troops, or troops being exposed to devastating enemy fire because units are advancing at different speeds. We even have to have some knowledge of tactics and weaponry, as we might have to decipher garbled military jargon that is of vital importance. We have been given some demonstrations by soldiers to prepare us.

There are some soldiers who are doubtful that we can

do the job. "Women giving battle orders!" they say in disbelief. We will show them.

July 20

It is getting hot and the U.S. military is beginning to build up. It is so dusty we wear masks over our faces for some relief. I feel we're headed toward something big. I'm working as hard as I can to ensure that I am asked to move forward when they need us even closer to the front. I have become quite an efficient switchboard operator, you know. I wonder what Mrs. Walker would think of that — I went off to war, became a telephone operator, and fell in love with a doughboy. Francie will be thrilled! I'll write to her now.

August 3

Nothing new to write today. Working very hard. We are all extremely tired and hotter than I've ever been. Alice is looking quite pale, but says she is fine. I can tell she is not for she has stopped joking around all the time and hardly laughs at all. I guess we have all stopped our fooling around and now take this work more seriously than we have so far. The heat is taking the life out of us but we go on proudly, hoping we can make a difference in winning this war and getting our troops safely out of danger.

August 10

The army is moving in all around us. Every day we see more doughboys passing through in a convoy of army trucks. I find myself half hoping that I will see Will or Sam in one of those trucks, and half hoping that they are in a safer place. But, if I know them, they aren't safe at all. They're headed right toward the action.

In the distance, there is a rumble of the disturbing noises war makes and I wonder what is planned.

August 12

Today was like a nightmare. For a few days Alice has been looking pale and even a little clammy, but when I ask her to get herself checked, she refuses. She is so stubborn! She wouldn't even take a rest for the day. She just kept saying that she was not here to lie in a bed. So, today we were heading back to our quarters after a long shift and Alice was looking just awful. Beads of sweat were forming on her forehead with every step we took. Finally, I grabbed her hand because she looked like she might fall. And thank goodness, because the moment I had her hand, the weight of her body fell right on me and we both fell to the ground.

She wasn't responding at all, even as I shouted her name. Her eyes were closed and she was still as can be. I got myself out from under her and looked around, but saw no one. There was nothing I could do but try and get her to the infirmary all by myself. I squatted down and put her arms over my shoulders and picked up the rest of her so that she was lying in my arms like a baby. I was so scared. I was so afraid that she wouldn't be okay that I hardly noticed the weight of her. I simply walked. Fast.

Well, we finally arrived and I was sweating so much and breathing so heavily I could barely speak. I shouted "Help us!" with all the breath I could muster and two nurses ran to our aid. It all happened very fast after that. They worked on her while I sat there and rested. And prayed. As hard as I could, I prayed that Alice would be all right. My eyes were burning with tears when the nurse finally came to tell me that Alice was okay . . . for now. She had gotten influenza, and she had waited so long without treatment that she was in critical condition. Then the nurse told me that there were no beds for Alice here because so many injured soldiers had come in today.

I looked at the beds — all of them full — and I panicked. I just let go. I was sobbing — sobbing because I was tired of working so hard, because I was so lonely for Maman, because I have been so far from home for so long already. And I was sobbing for all those boys lying in beds, injured and maybe dying, and any one of them could have been Will. Or Sam. But mostly, I was crying because Alice was sick and I was scared and very, very tired.

Then this young man, this wonderful doughboy, he sat up in his bed with bandages over both of his eyes and said, "She must take my bed, ma'am. Please, give her my bed. I'll sit in a chair, okay? It's only my eyes after all. Why waste a whole bed?" With that, I was stunned back into reality. I felt terrible for making him get up, but I had to agree.

We got Alice settled into the bed quickly. Here it is August, and we were piling Alice's shivering body with blankets. Her eyes were open now, but she wasn't really looking at me. I'm not sure she even knew who I was. I just sat with her. I held her hand, gave her as much water as she would take, and sponged the dampness off her head. And I prayed some more. The nurses sent me home to get some rest. (They had tried to keep me away from her, fearing that I would fall ill as well. But they gave up their fight pretty quickly once they saw that I wouldn't even consider it.)

So here I am, back in my quarters, writing with the shakiest of writing just to put some of these details away so that I might sleep. Until this moment, I had treated this as an adventure. A daydream we might have concocted in the kitchen. Tonight, though, this is real. I am in Neufchâteau, France, operating a switchboard, relaying orders to the men who fight this war. Perhaps somewhere deep inside the dream I dreamed of leaving New York City to do something different than the others, I knew this might get bad. Of course I knew. I just never knew how it would feel.

August 13

Alice is only a very little bit improved. I had to work today, of course, but I went to the infirmary on my way there. Alice was sleeping. But, when I went again this evening, she was awake. I sat with her, not saying too much of anything. Then she whispered my name and asked me to do her a favor. "Simone. Will you please write to my family?" I told her that she could write them when she was feeling better. But she put her hand on mine and looked hard at me. "I think that might not happen, Simone. Now, please do this for me. I have some things to say. Please." My heart fell into my stomach, but looking at her, I knew she was right. In just one day, she must have lost a quarter of her body weight and her skin was turning ashen. I got some paper and let her dictate to me.

It was so lovely, her letter. She said a kind thing to each and every one of her brothers. But to all of them she said, "Now don't think that because I am not there that I cannot see you. I will be watching over all of you and making sure that you are kind and good always and that others are kind and good to all of you. I will see to it." I should like to meet Alice's family one day. They must be a wonderful family to have Alice love them so much.

August 14

Alice is gone. I mailed her letter.

August 15

This is a terrible time. There is no time for mourning in war, you know. We must all work hard not to break down while we are handling the lines. The others are sad, too, of course. But I feel so lonely that I cannot catch my breath. Tonight I went for a walk and decided to write a letter of my own to Alice's family. I thought it might help them to know what kind of daughter they had, and I thought it might help me to remember her in writing. I've put it down here as part of my record of this experience that has suddenly turned grim.

> *To the Kealy Family,*
>
> *I am Simone Spencer, one of the girls in your daughter Alice's Signal Corps unit. I am writing so that you might have something more personal right now than that dreadful telegram our army must have delivered. I feel compelled to tell you that Alice was a gift to me. I never had a sister —*

and never knew I wanted one — until I met Alice. I came here not knowing one single thing about anything outside of my little neighborhood in New York City. I only knew I wanted to know more, and I wanted to help. Alice, too. With her, I was braver and better than I would have been all by myself. She told me stories about your neighborhood and your wonderful family. She must have mentioned each of you at least one thousand times a day. I hope one day I will meet you all. I would like to know some more Kealys in this lifetime.

My very deepest condolences,
Simone Spencer

I will never forget you, Alice Kealy.
Goodnight.

August 20

I haven't been able to write very much. Truly, I haven't really wanted to. But things are heating up now and I want to put it all down here. There is long-range artillery nearby and as a result we have become even more important than before. The major military buildup continues and you can feel suspense in the air. It's like reading a book and having no idea how it will end, but hoping it will go the way you're praying for!

Frantic calls come in all the time now. The orders have gone from being clearly spoken to being shouted, and the voices sound shaky at best. Where are Will and Sam? I try not to think too much about where they are headed, but sometimes I cannot help but worry for them.

September 1

They need hello girls to serve at the front! Orders have come for just six girls to move with the advance echelon of First Army. Everyone has offered to go, of course. Miss Banker has been chosen, since she has been in charge of us all along and since she is far and away the very best of any of us. She was then put in charge of choosing whom she would bring with her and I am among them!

September 5

We have left Neufchâteau and I couldn't be more relieved. Superstition says that if you look back on a place you are leaving, you will not return to it. I looked back on this place where my friend died as we pulled away in the truck. I looked back at it until it was out of my sight completely.

I have a purpose now. To do my job and get back home.

September 8

We are in the new headquarters in Ligny-en-Barrois, a town only a few miles from St. Mihiel, which is where all of the noise and chaos has been coming from lately. I believe it is where General Pershing is preparing our army to attack and push the Germans back. I also believe it is where Will and Sam must be. This will be the first American-led battle. Until this point, the Americans have been reinforcing the exhausted French soldiers.

We have taken up our duties in a house on the main street here. Sandbags are piled high outside. Inside there are a few switchboards behind which are piled rolls of wire and kegs of nails. At first, some of us sat on packing boxes until more chairs and desks could be rounded up, but now we are properly situated at our stations.

We are only five miles from the front! This is really the first time that it feels like we are in the war zone, like we might be in danger ourselves. Here, we watch as even more trucks rumble by, filled with troops and artillery. This goes on day and night and it's hard to get sleep. Tonight we walked out to a French observation post and we could see the flares over the trenches.

I feel very lonely here without Alice, without knowing what will happen next. How did I get here? I haven't heard from Maman in weeks and I'm sure it's because we've moved so much recently. In her last letter she told me that all the news at home says we're getting close to victory. We'd better get there fast because I'm beginning to lose my nerve.

September 10

Everyone is excited for the drive to begin. We are trying to take St. Mihiel back from the Germans, who have been blocking rail transport through there since 1914. It is *our* job to make sure no order goes unheard. Special lines called operation lines have been put on our switchboards to be used only in connection with the drive.

I'm trying to keep my spirits up. The others have been

very kind. We're all in this together after all. They remind me that this is why I came, to make a difference. It is very thrilling indeed to sit at the board and feel the importance of it now.

Still, I can't help but be afraid. I fear that the connections will not be made in time. I worry about each passing second. Hopefully, all the training, all the experience I've had so far won't fail me now. I do wish I had my angel. I hope that angel has enough power to watch over all three of us. Or at least just Will and Sam — from what I can tell, they're the ones who are truly in danger.

September 16

We have liberated St. Mihiel! The night the drive began we were called to the exchange office. Until then, only the men had been operating the switchboards through the night. For the three days of the attack, we were on four hours and off four hours. We worked day and night, but even though it was incredibly straining, and all the officers were on edge, even though it was quite difficult to keep our tempers in check as everything came in at once, even though the lines would go out of order because of the bombs or because of the thunderstorms that rained down during the offensive — well, in spite of all of this, we were excited and efficient and we did it! I did it!

We worked in those broken shifts, handling an average of 40,000 words a day through eight lines leading out of Ligny. There was incredible noise from our newest weapon — our armored tank — and I was taking calls from headquarters and yelling the orders over the lines to those boys in the trenches. I think if I had stopped for one moment during those shifts, I might have panicked. So I plugged on.

Things did get confusing to be sure. As usual, so much of the work was in codes to make sure the enemy could not tell where our army is, but the codes were changing almost as soon as we got them. Ligny was "waterfall," the Fourth Corps was known as "Nemo," at least for a while. If anyone had happened upon this room in the midst of the battle, if they had stopped to listen to us for a minute, they might just have thought we had gone perfectly mad. They might have thought we were screaming at one another in a sanitarium instead of an office of war. But then, in war, we all do go a little mad.

In any case, as the enemy was being pushed out of St. Mihiel by our powerful First Army, it became easier to stick to our tasks. We were going along smoothly

when, all of a sudden, the voices that had been screaming orders at us eased. Now the messages coming in over
the lines were not so harsh. Some even said funny things.
It was from the sound of their laughter, from the sigh of
relief their voices breathed, that we knew the drive had
been a success. And we looked around at one another,
dirty with dust and sweaty from stress, and we gave ourselves a small cheer. We girls were the only communications link from headquarters to the fighting in and
around St. Mihiel. I can't believe it myself! Alice should
have been here for this. It is the very reason she came. It's
the reason we all came.

I think I will finally be able to sleep tonight.

P.S. I forgot to mention one little thing. One of the
most exciting parts now of all this is watching the
prison pen fill up with German soldiers.

September 20

Well, our doughboys continue to hammer at the
Hindenburg Line, a fortified line of trenches, trying to
tire out the Germans and get them to give up their fight,
but we are on the move again with the First Army head-

quarters — off to Souilly. I do hope it will be home until the end. And I hope the end comes soon. I can't believe that we are nearing the end of September now.

I finally heard from home. Maman and Father both wrote a section of the letter and I was so calmed by the fact that life goes on as usual for them. Maman says the leaves are beginning to turn colors and that she misses me more when the seasons change. I know what she means. The change from one season to the next can be lonely when you're missing someone.

Francie even stuck in a note telling me to get home fast and to bring her a soldier, too! Mrs. Walker thinks she has found Francie the perfect husband and she's counting on me to get her out of it!

I've heard from a senior officer that Will's unit is among those we communicate with, and that his unit has been vital to the victories so far. He says they will be crucial in the next drive, too. Have I heard his voice over those lines? Have I spoken to Sam?

September 26

We have traveled through Bar-le-Duc to Souilly where we (plus one more girl they sent from Neufchâteau) finally arrived to find a small, shell-torn village. We have taken over the Armée Adrienne barracks, along with some old wooden sheds that are remnants of when the French held the fortress of Verdun against the assaults of the Germans very early on in the war. It was here that the bloodiest battle of this war was fought, between the French and the Germans in 1916.

We found the barracks lined with old newspapers and maps — to keep out the cold, I suppose. Thank goodness the YWCA has come to our aid once again with blankets and oilcloths. It is getting very cold. I shudder to think that we will lose more men still, and that my dear brother, and my dear Sam, could be among them.

October 1

Though we are in a sea of mud, we have acquired a sitting room that has a piano! It was taken from a German dugout. Who can imagine that they'd leave such a thing behind? The 27th Engineers helped us get settled — they even made us shelves and wash stands. Instead of glass windows, we have the kind that might be more likely found in a chicken coop — the kind you can prop up with a stick for light and air during the day. We shut them tight at night and cover them with black cloth to keep our presence and whereabouts a secret from the Germans. There are dugouts for shelter and one in particular very far into the ground where a single switchboard stands — ready for any emergency.

We are truly in an advance area. We can see the red glare from the shelling and feel the reverberations caused by the booming of the big guns. Right now we are only in charge of the operating boards. In fact, the calls we handle are so routine, there are moments when I have to remind myself why I'm here. After all, we handle supply and transportation matters — these are hardly the kinds of things we were shouting over the lines in Ligny. I feel like I've been demoted!

October 10

Not for long! Now we must handle the entire exchange, which includes the fighting lines. These connect the fighting units with the commanders who are directing their movements. Can you believe that every order given, every order for troop movement — they all come over these lines?

October 15

Six more girls have arrived to relieve us a bit. It is nice to have more time in between shifts. However, it hasn't stopped raining and it is quite cold and very damp, so there isn't much to do but rest a little. It is barely October and it feels like winter already. There is ice on the water pails each morning and Miss Banker's feet even froze! She had just gone to bed when a leak in the roof began to bother her. Though she tried to move her bed several times to avoid it, more leaks seemed to follow her. Poor Miss Banker — she cannot wear shoes at all now! She does not complain. Not one word. She is quite right when she says that we are much better off than those boys in the trenches.

Christmas is getting closer, and I feel further from it than ever before.

October 20

Although we don't know how many soldiers we've lost in this offensive, we've heard the numbers are in the tens — maybe hundreds — of thousands. For weeks we have been operating two field switchboards from this cold, leaking Signal Corps exchange, and we are freezing cold and tired. The battle goes on. It is loud over the lines. I listen closely for two voices I long to hear.

October 29

The constant thunder of heavy guns precludes any sleep. German air attacks are a daily occurrence all around us and we must work day and night to keep our boys informed. No one misses a shift here and work on the switchboard causes so much anxiety in us that our nerves are shattered. The advancing armies constantly change field positions and every new location requires a code change.

It is like it was during the St. Mihiel drive, only so much more goes wrong here and it feels so very grave. Connections to the front are maintained only after much difficulty. Then frantic, desperate calls come in on the wrong lines and you don't know what to do with them. We try to let them know that they have the wrong connection, but they can hardly hear us — we can hardly hear ourselves. We disconnect the calls then and hope they eventually find what they needed. Hope they found it in time.

The excitement of St. Mihiel was that the drama was new for us, and then that the battle was won so fast. This one feels like it will never end.

October 30

What a terrible day. It was noon and we were dealing with heavy traffic on the lines when a fire broke out in one of the old barracks buildings. The flames spread until they consumed eight buildings — including our own Signal Corps center! Everyone worked like mad around us, but the fire was unstoppable. The flames were horrifying — we could see them spreading in our direction, but we could not leave our switchboards. We *would* not.

We did not get up from our posts until we were literally threatened with disciplinary action. We returned just one hour later only to find that most of our lines had been cut by the fire. It was sad and very exasperating to see what we were up against, but there was nothing we could do but get back to operating the lines that still worked. Thank goodness the army headquarters had just moved to another barracks, so it was saved.

Later, we were allowed to return to gather any belongings we could find from our burned quarters. I found my diary, buried under some blankets that must have kept it safe. Now it smells of smoke. That's okay with me. When I am back in my room, in my luxurious room, I will lift this book to my nose to remember this experience. And I will be ever grateful for it. I just pray that when I get back to my room, everything will be as it was, and that we will all be safe and sound and together!

We were moved into new quarters — in an unfinished shed. We're just fine though. No complaints at all. I don't know when it happened, but somewhere along the way, we have become soldiers.

November 1

We have broken through the German defenses at Meuse. We are on our way now, I'm sure! I must run to the office.

November 11

The war is over!

This day was so strange — the traffic coming over the lines was heavier than it has been in recent weeks, especially artillery traffic. And then, very suddenly at 11

A.M. this morning, the guns simply went silent. We were told first of all that they had declared an armistice. America has won! And so have France and England and Russia!

We were told to celebrate quietly, and we have been instructed to maintain a low profile among the French. No America boasting allowed! I don't think anyone paid too much attention to this mandate since there was a band concert in the village when we went out tonight. For the first time, we didn't have to pay attention to "blackouts."

November 12

The wounded keep coming in, and everywhere there are wounded soldiers with bloodied faces and missing limbs. Yes, missing limbs. The ones who survive their amputations will have to go home without entire pieces of their bodies. The rest of us will go home without pieces of ourselves, too. But our missing pieces will be less obvious.

I haven't yet seen Will or Sam. Where could they be? I am very afraid. I feel sure that they would have come in by now. Some people are off to Paris and I heard some of the troops will be headed there. Perhaps that's where I'll find them. I think I will go there. At least from Paris, I can find my own way home.

November 17

I am in Paris and feel more lost than ever. A group of us came here together — others stayed behind to work the lines through the transition out of war. Some will stay in Paris and work, too. Everyone is in a glorious state except me.

There are Red Cross dances most every night, and I go to each one without even looking at myself in a mirror, just to see if they are there. Things are so different now. I liked it better when we spent a good long time doing ourselves up for a dance. I liked it better when Alice was right beside me with her arm in mine when we walked inside. I liked it when Will was there. I even liked it better when Sam was being terrible. I would take it all right now. I'm sorry to say it, but I would go right back to being at war if only I could have my brother back safely and my dear Alice and Sam, too.

I walked by a Y hut tonight that had a Victrola playing my song. Our song.

December 1

I have spent the last two weeks helping out as much as I possibly can, but now I have begged my way onto a ship headed for New York. I am going home. Alone. I was able to wire Maman and Father that I would arrive in New York on the sixteenth of December, but I have heard nothing back from them. I imagine someone would have told me if something had happened to Will. Maman would surely know by now and they would have sent for me. No news is good news is what everyone tells me, so I will board this ship with only cheerful thoughts of a reunion. I will pray for it the whole way home.

December 8

I ask around if anyone knows William Spencer or Samuel Cates and every single answer is "No, Miss." This ship is filled with wounded men and Red Cross workers. The journey home isn't a thing like the journey here. The soldiers are very proud of themselves of course, for winning this war once and for all. But there is something somber in the air. It makes me think that no matter what they say, no one really wins a war.

December 16

I am simply exhausted but had to write down the most incredible events of this day. I am home and New York City has never looked as glorious as it did when we docked this afternoon. I held my breath when I walked down the plank, hoping that someone would be there to greet me. But I was nearly the last one off, and by then, the cheering had died down and so had the crowd. I searched the crowd with tired eyes for a familiar face, truly thinking that I would have to find someone to take me home. I was thinking that I would have to ring my very own doorbell and hope that my parents had stayed in this night.

Then, all of a sudden, they appeared. There was Maman and Father and Will, too! I ran to them, and fell into them hugging and kissing them with every last bit of energy I had. It was such a big mess of a reunion that we all fell on top of one another right onto the ground! I was relieved to see Will most of all. I didn't even try to stand up again. I just sat there hugging him around the neck, sobbing so hard I couldn't speak. Will held on tightly to me, crying a little bit. I was happier at that moment than I had been since the first night I saw Will in Chaumont.

I will write more later after I spend a good long time taking in my family. Caroline is here and Sally has prepared a feast! What a joy it is to be home.

Later

Will says Sam is dead. He says that he didn't make it out of the Meuse-Argonne Offensive. He says Sam was there one minute and gone the next. They were side by side when an explosion occurred on a charge and all Will can remember was being carried away by two other doughboys. He says he was shouting for Sam, but they told him he didn't make it. Will had suffered a concussion in that explosion and woke up in an army hospital. He asked about Sam and no one knew where he was taken. Everyone thought he had died. Will was sent home soon after that because he could no longer fight. He tells me all this and still I don't shed a tear.

He even gave me part of the angel that one of the others found near Sam that day. I hold in my hand part of the angel I gave Sam, and still I will not cry. He is not dead. He can't be.

December 17

Maman keeps trying to console me, thinking that I am in mourning, but I am not and so I find it very irritating. She says she believes me, that she will have faith with me, but I can tell by the way she looks at me that she does not.

Francie came by today and was intent on telling me all about her escapades since I've been gone, plus she wanted to hear every detail about the war and every word of my love story with Sam. She is a good friend to me. If she doesn't believe me that Sam is alive, she is a much better actress than I thought! Speaking of acting, I forgot to mention that I had several letters from Thomas waiting for me when I got home. I hadn't thought of him in such a long while and it is nice to know he was thinking of me. Imagine, I never even told him I left. He has no idea that in all this time, I have been to war and back again. I will write to him when I feel better. He was a soldier in this very same war and now he lives in sunny California and works for a movie studio called Universal City — the very same one that Mary Pickford works for. I bet he was trying to get as far away from the war as possible.

Later

Father has tried to find some information about Sam's family, hoping to find them and get some news. He told me there is no Cates family in New York with a son who went to the war. Then Will remembered that Sam's mother worked for the Gardners so they must know where she is. Father has called Mr. Gardner for the information. I'm sure this will all be settled soon and it will all have been a mistake. For now, it is very lonely being the only one who knows that Sam is okay.

Later still

I am lost. Father found out from the Gardners that Sam's mother and father died years ago, in a fire on the Lower East Side where they lived. They said Sam must have been just a little boy when it happened. Mr. Gardner said they don't have any idea what became of him. Why didn't Sam tell me? Did he try and I quieted him? Was I too afraid to hear how he had lived?

Tomorrow I will go to that address, 88 Orchard Street. Tomorrow I will find out more.

December 18

I went to the house where Sam lived. Max dropped me at the corner and waited while I looked around. 88 Orchard Street. It wasn't the house of a family. It was a home for boys. An orphanage. It was just awful down there. Laundry hanging from windows, weary-looking women huddled together as they walked down the street in thin coats. I think it is colder there. I think I know what Sam was getting at when he said things were different for him. I had no idea at all.

I sat on a stoop for a minute to collect myself and as the night fell, my thoughts turned darker. According to Will, he was hurt near the beginning of the Meuse-Argonne Offensive. That was almost three months ago. Surely I would have heard from Sam by now if he were all right.

I am losing hope. What if he really is gone? I am beginning to feel a pain in my heart that hurts like it did when Alice died. I know why it is called a broken heart. I know why people make up stories instead of writing journals of their lives. You just wouldn't write a story about two people who find each other and lose each other before they were ever given a little chance to love each other.

Maman held me tight when I got home. I cried tears of sadness now. I cried for Sam.

December 20

I have come from the hospital — the ward is filled with injured soldiers. It is hardly the place it was when Thomas was there. He was one of only a few. But Thomas did find his way out of that bed and so will many others. Katherine, the reconstruction aide who helped Thomas so much, is still there. She said she finally did get a letter from Thomas, too, and a few more after that. She is going to take me under her wing, for I told her all about Sam and how I just can't be at home right now pretending to have Christmas cheer. Katherine told me she understands it well and she thinks spending some time here again will help me heal.

The idea of trying to help these boys put themselves back together again encourages me. Watching Katherine work with them, physically putting one leg in front of the other for them, is the most exhilarating thing I've done since Ligny. It is what I must do now. I must help get them going again.

I came home this very cold afternoon into a house filled with the smells of Christmas once again. The tree is decorated, Sally bakes ginger cookies, and their scent wafts through this house causing it to smell like the Christmas shop of last year. Only I cannot enjoy even one minute of the festivities.

All around me, Christmas is happening just like we planned. We are all together, just like Maman said we would be. Last year at this time, all I wanted was to help my country and to make it home safely. I thought that was all I could ask for.

December 24

I think I have just about enough energy left to write down what happened to me on this most remarkable day. I have pinched myself more than once, hoping it would hurt so that this could not be a dream. It hurt every time. It isn't a dream — it just feels like one.

I was working at the hospital this afternoon, avoiding my house for the fourth day in a row. I was changing the sheets on a recently vacated bed when Katherine came over and asked me for a favor. She said she needed some help with a patient who had "Thomas Brennan Syndrome." I laughed at her because, of course, I knew that she meant this boy would speak to no one, just like Thomas. I told her I would stop in after Christmas but that I really ought to go home to be with my family on Christmas Eve. She wouldn't let me leave, though. She said she thought my time would be better spent helping out an injured and shell-shocked doughboy on Christmas Eve than it would be moping around the house. I thought she was right. When I walked into the room and looked toward the end of the long row of beds, I had no idea that the doughboy in that last bed by the window would be Sam.

Yes, it's true. It was Sam. When I imagined this moment in my head (a million times), I always thought I'd run to him and let him swing me around in celebration. But I didn't run over to him now. I had to suck in my breath and some tears because Sam was not standing, ready to swing me around. He was lying in a bed. He was badly injured. I felt Katherine give me a little push and she whispered to me that it was all right, that I should go over to him. So I gathered myself and picked up my pace until I almost ran toward him. I yelled his name in the quiet and he turned his head away from the window he'd been staring out of and toward me. I heard him say my name and he smiled. I put all my manners aside and leaned over to hug and kiss him. I cried again, but out of relief at last!

Once I had wiped away my tears and sat down in the chair beside his bed, I started to bombard him with questions. Where had he been? Why did everyone think he was dead? Why didn't he tell me about his parents? About his life? But mostly, I wanted to know why he hadn't tried to contact me.

I am still getting over the shock of what came next. He said that he had been knocked unconscious by that explosion and that the two soldiers who carried Will away thought he was dead. But soon, others came by and carried him to a hospital tent where they worked for hours to try and save his leg. They could not. Sam lifted the sheet to reveal his war wound. He had no leg from the knee down. I think I paused a moment too long when he showed me, because he quickly covered it up again and put his head back heavily on the pillow. Then he closed his eyes and told me that this was the reason he didn't try to find me. This was the very reason he did not want to be found. He wanted me to remember him strong and able, not crippled like this. I thought about that for a minute and sighed rather loudly. Then I said, "You're just as arrogant as ever, Sam Cates. You thought you knew me then and you were wrong. Why would you trust yourself to make another decision about me? I don't think you're any different at all, as a matter of fact. Same old Sam."

He smiled then and squeezed my hand and I stayed there until I had to go home and report the news. I told him I'd be back to visit tomorrow.

When I got home, I slammed the front door extra hard so everyone would come running and when they did, I practically screamed out my news. Will didn't believe me at first. I think he had done such a good job of convincing himself that Sam was gone that he never thought to hope for this. But when I told them the whole story, Will started to come around. In fact, he grabbed his coat and ran out the door shouting that he had to go see his friend for himself. Caroline and Maman were stunned and excited and they hurried me into the parlor to sit and talk with them some more.

Somehow, though, I think Father was the most relieved of all of them. From the sofa, I could see him standing in the foyer with his head in his hands. Perhaps he understood my pain most of all. Perhaps he had considered what it might have been like to never know Maman beyond their very first moments together in Paris.

Later

Will has returned from the hospital. They only allowed him to see Sam for a minute, but he plans to return with me tomorrow. He said good night then, and he was about to close the door to my room when he turned around and apologized for losing faith. I told him that I don't think he ever did lose faith, that he was just trying to move on. Deep down, I don't think either of us had given up on Sam.

December 25

I couldn't have asked for a lovelier Christmas. I had planned to go to the hospital right after our lunch to see Sam again. Maman and the others were going to come, too. Everyone, including Sally, wanted to meet this love of mine. But my very sneaky Father found a better way!

He must have slipped out just as we were beginning to open presents because one minute I was clearing some space by the tree for everyone to sit and the next, I was looking right into the eyes of Sam, who had been wheeled in by Father, who was standing behind him. Father said that the hospital was no place for Sam to celebrate Christmas. I first ran into Father's arms to thank him for this wonderful gift. (He must have broken a lot of rules to get Sam out of there today!) Then, I took Sam's hand and introduced him to everyone. Maman gave him a kiss on each cheek and welcomed him home.

Then, Sam pulled me down toward him and showed me his other hand, which he had made into a fist. I was puzzled for a moment, but then he opened it and there it was in his palm. My angel. The missing part of my angel. Sam had carried it with him the whole time. I took it from him and pulled some string from an unopened present under the tree to make a hook.

Carefully, I hung it, broken but beautiful, on the strongest pine branch I could find, just where it belongs. On the Spencer Christmas tree.

January 1, 1919

I am nineteen today and I almost forgot to celebrate. I have been to the hospital every day since Christmas, cheering for Sam as Katherine trains him to walk again. She has started him on crutches and I must say it is a relief to see him standing tall again. I am so inspired by her that I have decided to formally train as a reconstruction aide once things calm down. For now, I will work at that hospital, helping any boy who needs me.

I was sitting with Sam this evening after his therapy when I noticed a glow coming from the hallway. Then, Maman walked in carrying a cake lit with candles, singing softly in French, "Bon Anniversaire à vous . . ." Behind her stood the entire family and Francie, too. As they approached, Sam took my hand and my heart swelled.

As we sat there, eating cake and telling stories, I realized that this was my happy ending. Had I written it myself, I couldn't have made it better. I would have scratched out all the aching and the crying, tossing those sad pages into the trash bin. And then who would appreciate the ending, where I'm sitting in a hospital room, and I've lost a dear friend, and my Sam has lost his leg, and all I can think is that I am blessed?

The thing is, if in your life, you never got any bad news, never got weary, never got the wind knocked out of you, well, there would be nothing left in this world to move you. And there would be no reason at all to well up in a teary smile and hold on tight to everything you love. I know now that that's the whole point. That's the whole point of everything.

Epilogue

Simone Spencer married Samuel Cates in Central Park on May 25, 1920. Their wedding song was "Till We Meet Again." Perhaps their dance was a bit less graceful than their first, but it was no less meaningful. (Simone had trained as a reconstruction aide and practiced on Sam until he could walk with an artificial leg and a cane.) He was dashing as always.

Sam went to work for Will, who had taken over Grandfather's real estate business. The Roaring Twenties were filled with parties and laughter for the Cates's and the Spencers. Sam and Simone eventually moved to Boston, where Sam attended Harvard Law School. One day, just after they'd arrived, Simone summoned up the courage to pay a visit to the Kealy family. She was taken aback by the resemblance of Mrs. Kealy to her old friend Alice. She met the whole family that one day. In and out they came, showing her pictures, sharing stories, sharing memories, of Alice.

Years went by, and the stock market crash of 1929 brought economic hardship to Simone and her family. Will had made the mistake of investing nearly all the money in the stock market, and the only real estate they had left was the original Spencer home. Sam and Simone moved home to New York City where Sam worked as an advocate for struggling immigrants and Simone continued to work as a physical therapist at the Hospital for Special Surgery, once called the Hospital for the Ruptured and Crippled.

Between Sam and Simone and Will and Caroline, the Spencer home filled up with children. Maman and Father found the crowd a bit much, and at long last they moved to Paris, where they would live out the rest of their years.

Francie went to California to become an actress. On the set of a movie, she bumped right into the man she would marry, Mr. Thomas Brennan, who had a starring role.

Once the economy recovered, Will and Caroline moved to the suburbs, and Sam and Simone and their three children had the house all to themselves. When

America entered World War II, Simone and her children planted a victory garden outside and volunteered regularly at the Y. This time, Simone was content to stay home, with her family and her memories.

Once their children were grown, Sam and Simone moved to Paris where they, too, lived out their days. They were buried alongside Simone's grandparents and parents in an overgrown cemetery at the end of a winding city street.

Life in America
in 1917

Historical Note

In 1914, some of the most powerful nations in Europe went to war, while America stayed silent. It was not our war. In fact, it was to be a short war, fought over just a few months. Many thought peace would return by 1915. But, as the battles raged on, it became clear that more was at stake. Germany, France, Russia, Italy, and Great Britain would fight until someone was victorious. It was to be "the war to end all wars."

America's perspective changed in 1917, when a German telegram was intercepted on its way to Mexico. In it, Germany promised to help Mexico get back some of the land it had lost to America, if Mexico would align itself against the United States. On April 6, 1917, America declared war on Germany and joined the Allied forces of France and England.

America's involvement in World War I helped the Allies regain some power in numerous violent battles with the Germans. Regarded as the first modern war, this was the first time industrial as well as human resources were utilized in battle. Besides the infamous trench warfare, there were chemical weapons, armored tanks, machine guns, airplanes, and submarines — all combined to yield a tragic amount of casualties.

Something else that distinguished the first World War, though, was that women were enlisted to ease the burden of having so many men fighting in the trenches. In England, thousands of women enlisted in Queen Mary's Women's Auxilliary Army Corps (WAAC) and the Volunteer Aid Detachment (VAD), which put women to work as munitions workers, farmers, cooks, and nursing assistants. In France, hundreds of thousands of women signed up to be "munitionettes." For the first time, governments were seeing the value of allowing women to contribute to the war effort. It would open doors for women even after the war ended.

The United States, however, remained reluctant to utilize women in the same way. Although the U.S. Navy enrolled women as yeomen, and later the Marine Corps saw the benefit of involving women to offset the shortage of clerical assistance, the U.S. Army would not sanction it.

American women would not be deterred. They found other ways to contribute, other ways overseas. Some went with the Y.W.C.A., others with the Red Cross, and still more with the Salvation Army. Even as the suffrage movement was in full force in America, the effort of the women who supported the war did wonders for earning women the respect they deserved.

By the time America entered the war, women's roles had been changing for quite some time. In cities like New York, women were organizing for better working conditions in the factories, the suffrage movement was getting louder, and, in small enclaves left over from the Gilded Age of New York, very wealthy women were looking for more. Indeed, their lives had changed, too. The "old money" of the earliest settlers of the city — like the Vanderbilts and the Astors — no longer afforded the society set the stature they lived for. Instead, new waves of immigrants were beginning to make money in real estate and banking, all the while dissolving the gap between them and the very, very rich. An upper-middle class was developing.

So, for the first time, women who had once been

content to attend dinner parties and fancy balls now peered out the windows of their luxurious homes, looking for a way to contribute. It was a new time, indeed.

Then General John J. Pershing made a decision. After spending some time in France, readying American troops to fight the Germans, he realized that without proper communication between headquarters and the trenches, the Allies could not win. And the French telephone system simply would not do. He needed a quality, efficient communications network. He wanted bilingual operators. He wanted highly skilled operators. He wanted American operators. And he wanted them to be women. Having seen women fill the roles of men in England and France, Pershing had faith in his decision.

Late in 1917, a call went out. Recruiting was easy. Of the thousands that applied, only 150 were assigned to training, and a few hundred more held for reserves. All of the women who volunteered were trained in both telephone operating and military drills. Also, all of the women were sworn in, which led them to believe they were officers of the U.S. Army.

When they arrived in France, they were assigned to locations that ranged from quiet and calm to booming and dangerous — the latter was especially true as the war neared its end. The Signal Corps operators, or "hello girls" as the soldiers liked to call them, acted as both operators and as interpreters. Sometimes, in the most crucial moments, they would be responsible for interpreting an order, and relaying it to the men in the trenches. It was an enormous responsibility — and it was one the women took very seriously.

By the end of the war, 223 operators were sent overseas. They lived in rugged conditions, handled thousands of frantic calls, and boosted the morale of the soldiers with their kindness and efficiency. Many would say that they helped win the war. They were strong, smart women from all different backgrounds who had come together to make history.

Only when they returned to the United States, did they discover that they had been intentionally misled to believe they were officers in the U.S. Army. Ineligible for honorable discharge or medals for their service, the hello girls were simply considered contract employees of the Signal Corps. Though they had been sworn in, worn their uniforms proudly, and been subjected to military rules and disciplinary action, their contribution was going without notice on the home front.

Merle Egan Anderson, a former hello girl who had

been stationed at Tours during the war, began a fight for recognition that would last sixty years. At long last, in 1977, after more than fifty bills granting veteran status to the hello girls had been introduced in Congress but failed, a young lawyer named Mark Hough won the battle. Along with the Veterans of WWI, the Women's Overseas League, and an outspoken Senator from Arizona, Barry Goldwater, Hough got the hello girls approved for veteran status. It wasn't until 1979 that the girls who were still alive would receive the medals and benefits, not to mention the status, they deserved. By then, only eighteen survived.

When World War I was finally over, nearly ten million men had lost their lives on the battlefield. Twenty million were wounded. Due to the terrible battle injuries, the war also created a need for a new kind of medicine — physical "reconstruction," or rehabilitation. France and England already had reconstruction aide programs in place, so the American Expeditionary Force ordered a study of their programs. Soon programs were in place in this country and the physical therapy profession was born. At the time, physical and occupational therapy were about returning people to function after injury, limb loss, or paralysis. Mary McMillan, an early physical therapist, said, "The profession was born in response to a brand-new need."

When the armistice went into effect at 11 A.M. on November 11, 1918, the world was a different place. Europe had suffered a tremendous loss of human life as well as the destruction of its buildings and landscape. And there would be new political and cultural clashes to come. But with the end of the war there also came a hopeful time in America. Indeed, as this country headed into the Roaring Twenties, the economy soared, and, perhaps most remarkably, greater opportunities for women brought equality within our reach.

The lake in Central Park is filled with row boaters enjoying a pleasant spring or summer day in the early 1900s. At the time, Central Park was a popular spot for the fashionable upper classes to people-watch.

Millionaire's Row, a mile-long stretch of elegant houses on the Upper East Side of New York City, ran along Fifth Avenue. It was the center of high society in the early twentieth century. Many of the homes have since been converted into museums.

Two society women sport stylish hats and outfits as they walk along Fifth Avenue in New York City in 1918.

NEW YORK JOURNAL

EIGHTH EDITION
EIGHTH EDITION

House by a Vote of 373 to 50 Passes Joint Resolution

WAR IS DECLARED BY U. S.

Interned German Ships Seized by Customs Authorities

Washington, April 6.—After a debate of nearly seventeen hours, the House early to-day passed the resolution previously adopted in the Senate, declaring a state of war against the Government of Germany. The vote was 373 to 50.

The resolution now goes to Vice-President Marshall, who must sign it in formal session of the Senate. It will then be taken before the President for his signature.

Amendments to prevent the use of United States military forces in Europe, Asia or Africa unless directed by Congress were voted down. The resolution adopted by the Senate on Wednesday was accepted by the House without the dotting of an "i."

ESSELS IN ALLIES REST PORT HERE

BEFORE BIG DRIVE TAKEN

"LOVE U. S. BUT CAN'T VOTE FOR WAR"—MISS RANKIN

CZAR SUPPLIANT FOR PENSION TO DUMA

CARRANZISTAS MASSING ON BORDER

President's Historic Address Free to Journal Readers

AUSTRIA EAGER TO KEEP PEACE WITH U. S.

This headline of the New York Journal publicizes the U.S. declaration of war against Germany, marking America's entry into World War I in 1917.

General John J. Pershing, an army general who had earlier led many successful military operations, was selected by President Woodrow Wilson to command the United States military (called the American Expeditionary Force) in Europe during World War I.

A woman kisses good-bye an American soldier, or doughboy, as he boards a ship preparing to leave for the World War I battlefront in Europe.

157

General John J. Pershing ordered a unit of French-speaking American women, selected and trained by AT&T, to volunteer as switchboard operators on the Western Front in France during World War I. The young women, chosen from all over the United States, received telegrams (above) instructing them where and when to report for training. They were to be a part of the U.S. Army Signal Corps and came to be known by soldiers as "hello girls" (below).

Parisians and visitors alike sit along the Champs-Élysées in Paris, sipping coffee or simply people-watching, as crowds stroll past.

During World War I, the Louvre Museum in Paris was fortified with sandbags to protect the beautiful building and the precious artifacts inside from shelling and bomb blasts.

Often situated dangerously close to the battlefronts, the U.S. Army Signal Corps telephone operators worked switchboards all over the Western Front. Helmets and gas masks would hang behind their chairs in case of German shelling or gas attacks.

Two members of the U.S. Army Signal Corps sit in their quarters, sharing a letter. Despite the harsh conditions and great risk, the women found ways to make the situation bearable. They never complained.

The Young Women's Christian Association sent volunteers abroad during World War I to deliver supplies and to attend to American soldiers in the field hospitals (above). The YWCA also helped the troops by creating warm places for soldiers to relax (below).

A field hospital is set up in the bombed-out remains of a building in France. Bodies of the dead and wounded are lined up as doctors and nurses attend to them.

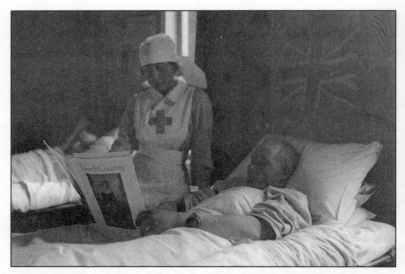

A Red Cross nurse reads a magazine to a wounded American soldier, by his bedside at a hospital in London.

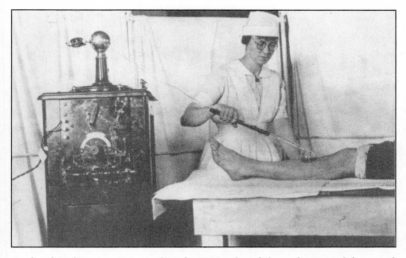

A relatively unknown profession in the early 1900s, physical therapy became vital during and after World War I. Therapists sent to hospitals in France were greeted with some degree of hostility. After sweeping floors and working as nurse's aides, therapists were finally allowed to work with wounded soldiers. Physical therapists employed techniques such as exercise, electrotherapy, and hydrotherapy (above). Occupational therapists helped wounded soldiers return to regular functioning with methods such as weaving (below), which encouraged them to use their injured hands.

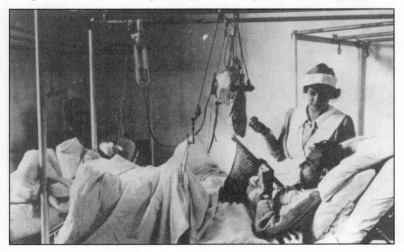

Many soldiers came home from World War I irreparably injured, sometimes with part or all of one of their legs amputated and requiring therapy in order to function again. Physical therapists helped them to learn new skills and taught them how to use artificial legs so that they could walk again.

French civilians and American soldiers celebrate Armistice Day on November 11, 1918, the day Germany surrendered, marking the victory of the Allied forces and the end of World War I.

OVER THERE

Johnnie, get your gun,
Get your gun, get your gun,
Take it on the run,
On the run, on the run.
Hear them calling, you and me,
Every son of liberty.
Hurry right away,
No delay, no delay,
Make your daddy glad
To have had such a lad.
Tell your sweetheart not pine,
To be proud her boy's in line.

Chorus:
Over there, over there,
Send the word, send the word over there —
That the Yanks are coming,
The Yanks are coming,
The drums rum-tumming
Ev'rywhere.
So prepare, say a pray'r,
Send the word, send the word to beware.
We'll be over, we're coming over,
And we won't come back till it's over
Over there.

Johnnie, get your gun,
Get your gun, get your gun,
Johnnie show the Hun
Who's a son of a gun.
Hoist the flag and let her fly,
Yankee Doodle do or die.
Pack your little kit,
Show your grit, do your bit.
Yankee Doodle fill the ranks,
From the towns and the tanks.
Make your mother proud of you,
And the old Red, White and Blue.

This song was written for the American soldiers fighting "over there" in Europe during World War I by George M. Cohan in 1917.

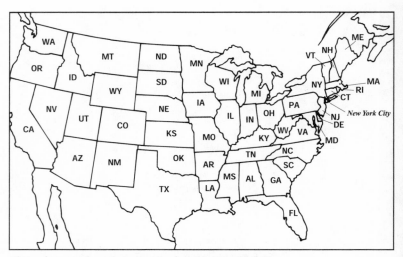

This modern map shows the approximate location of New York City.

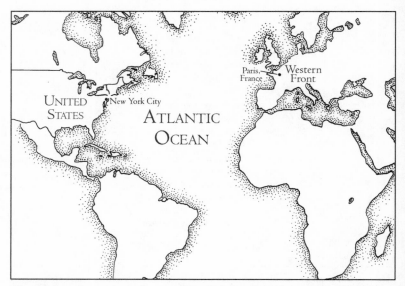

This map shows the approximate locations of New York City, Paris, France, and the Western Front.

About the Author

Beth Seidel Levine's inspiration for this book was her love of New York City. "I love New York," she says. "I especially love imagining it at different points in history. No matter how much research I do, I'm not sure I'll ever believe there was a time before subways and traffic jams, or a time when a hat was required attire for a lady! I wanted to capture what it felt like to live here when the city was in transition, when the lines between the classes were disappearing. 1917 was just that kind of year.

"America's entry into World War I provided a dramatic backdrop for the beginning of Simone's story. But to have her leave the city and abandon her luxurious lifestyle, she needed an awfully good reason. When I came across the story of the hello girls, I had found just the excuse Simone needed. Those woman answered the call to serve their country at a time when women couldn't even vote. They were so fearless and so very ahead of their time. Women like them paved the way for the rest of us. That is the real story."

Beth Seidel Levine lives in New York City. This is her first novel.

For giving me the best of everything,
for laughing the only way anyone should,
for letting me catch some of her spirit
and all of her love,
this book is for my mother,
Gail Seidel Levine.

Acknowledgments

Many, many thanks to Charles Levine, who is both a loving father and supportive friend; thanks to my dear brother Michael Levine, whom I adore and admire more than he will ever know; to my Reba, whose encouragement and unconditional love are unmatched; to my Grandmom Mimi, whose presence in my life is a blessing; to my Aunt Kris, Uncle Scott, Eliot, and Taylor, whose love and support define family; to the Ain Family for opening their home and their hearts to me. And most of all, my thanks go to Jonathan Ain, my love and my very best friend. I could not have done this without you. And to all my good friends — you all keep me going.

Thanks also to Amy Griffin, who handled the role of editor/cheerleader with as much support and guidance as she does the role of surrogate sister. And to Jean Feiwel for the opportunity of a lifetime (over and over again).

Thank you to Manuela Soares, Elizabeth Parisi, Kerrie Baldwin, Sarita Kusuma, Lisa Sandell, Diane Nesin, Dwayne Howard, and Amla Sangvhi. Together, you made this book come together.

Grateful acknowledgment is made for permission to reprint the following:

Cover Portrait: Portrait by J. B. Whitcomb, from the collection of Alan Johanson. Photograph from John Wood, The Art of the Autochrome.

Cover Background: Getty Images.

Page 97-98: "Till We Meet Again," words and music written by Raymond B. Egan and Richard Whiting in 1918.

Page 154 (top): Central Park, Brown Brothers.

Page 154 (bottom): Millionaire's Row, Brown Brothers.

Page 155: Socialites on Fifth Avenue, Brown Brothers.

Page 156 (top): Newspaper headline, Culver Pictures.

Page 156 (bottom): General Pershing, Bettman/CORBIS.

Page 157: Good-bye kiss, Culver Pictures.

Page 158 (top): Telegram, courtesy of the U.S. Army Communications-Electronics Museum, Fort Monmouth, N.J.

Page 158 (bottom): U.S. Army Signal Corps, courtesy of the U.S. Army Signal Corps via Sugar Moon Productions.

Page 159 (top): Café in Paris, Brown Brothers.

Page 159 (bottom): Louvre with sandbags, photo by Roger Viollet/Getty Images.

Page 160 (top): Signal Corps operators with gas masks and helmets, CORBIS.

Page 160 (bottom): Signal Corps Operations in quarters, CORBIS.

Page 161 (top): YWCA in field hospital, Brown Brothers.

Page 161 (bottom): Soldiers in cafeteria, Bettman/CORBIS.

Page 162 (top): Field hospital, Culver Pictures.

Page 162 (bottom): Nurse reads to solider, Getty Images.

Page 163 (top): Leg therapy, from the collection of Lettie Gavin, Seattle. Washington.

Page 163 (bottom): Soldier learning to weave, from the Archives of American Occupational Therapy Association, Bethesda, Maryland, courtesy of Lettie Gavin, Seattle, Washington

Page 164 (top): Amputees, from the collection of Lettie Gavin, Seattle, Washington.

Page 164 (bottom): Armistice Day, Getty Images.

Page 166: Maps by Heather Saunders.

Look for Dear America:

Christmas After All

The Great Depression Diary of Minnie Swift

Read this very special Dear America Christmas story set during the Great Depression in Indiana. Twelve-year-old Minnie Swift keeps a diary over the span of one Christmas month that reflects the sadness, but also the optimism that characterized this trying time in American history. It is the story of one family making it through difficult times with a persevering spirit. The Christmas Spirit.

Copyright © 2002 by Beth Seidel Levine

All rights reserved. Published by Scholastic Inc.
DEAR AMERICA®, SCHOLASTIC, and associated logos are trademarks
and/or registered trademarks of Scholastic Inc.

Library of Congress Cataloging-in-Publication Data
Levine, Beth Seidel.
When Christmas comes again : the World War I diary of Simone Spencer / by Beth Seidel Levine.
p. cm. — (Dear America)
Summary: Teenage Simone's diaries for 1917 and 1918 reveal her experiences as a carefree
member of New York Society, then as a "Hello girl," a volunteer switchboard operator for
the Army Signal Corps in France.
ISBN 0-439-43982-5
1. World War, 1914–1918 — New York (State) — Juvenile fiction. 2. World War, 1914–1918
France — Juvenile fiction. [1. World War, 1914–1918 — New York (State) — Fiction. 2. World War,
1914–1918 — France — Fiction. 3. Social classes — Fiction. 4. United States. Army. Signal Corps —
Fiction. 5. New York (N.Y.) — History — 20th century — Fiction. 6. Diaries — Fiction.]
I. Title. II. Series.
PZ7.L57826 Wh 2002
[Fic] — dc21   2002066987

10 9 8 7 6 5 4 3 2 1   02 03 04 05 06

The display type was set in Novella Bold.
The text type was set in Centaur MT.
Book design by Elizabeth B. Parisi
Photo research by Dwayne Howard and Amla Sanghvi

Printed in the U.S.A.   23
First edition, November 2002

DATE DUE

PRINTED IN U.S.A.